Furgotten Felonies

Sarah May Bird

To Auntie Jean and Uncle Martin

Contents

One

Latte in your hand
Purring felines by your feet
Cat Café heaven

"So, what do they do with it?" Oli asked, casting the cat tree a suspicious look as if it were about to reach out and trap him.

"Play with it. Climb on it. Scratch it," I said.

"Ignore it," Pippa suggested.

A soft sigh escaped my lips. "Yeah, sometimes they do that. You can buy your cat a wonderful expensive toy, and they'll still prefer the box it came in. Or your slippers."

"We spent," Oli checked the order slip. "~~Jesus bloody Christ~~, we spent *how* much on this thing?"

Pippa kissed him on the cheek and plucked the invoice from his hands. "It's a business investment, darling."

"And the baskets? And toys? And blankets? And bowls?" Oli listed off on his fingers. "Not to mention the food. All the food they're going to eat. So much food."

"Oli, it's a *cat* café," I said patiently. "It needs cats. Cats need this stuff to be happy. Happy cats mean happy customers. It'll pay for itself in no time."

"I wish it *would* pay for itself," Oli grumbled, lifting a small, feathered toy from one of the delivery boxes and giving it an experimental swish.

As confident as I tried to sound, my nerves were as frayed as my shoelaces after a cat had chewed them. While Oli scrutinised every purchase, my stomach twisted into a knot of anxiety. I re-ran the projected figures and went through the business plan in my head over and over to reassure myself.

It would work.

It would be a success.

And I would give a new, loving home to rescued cats and a haven for the spirits of dead cats.

Oh yes, did I forget to mention? I see dead cats.

They're drawn to me because they know I can see them and provide them with the love and attention their restless spirits crave in a world where their meows go unanswered by most humans.

"What," Oli asked, lifting a strange, floppy piece of material, "is this?"

"Uh, I think that's an octopus," Pippa said, running a slim finger down the invoice list. "Yes, octopus toy. You hang it up on one of the cat tree ledges and they bat the tentacles around."

Oli stared at the toy and shook his head. "Octopus. Of course. The natural enemy of *Felis Catus*."

Pippa snatched the toy from him and glared. A pen was stuck in the messy bun of her purple hair, and her jeans and pale blue top had fluff bunnies stuck to them from our deep cleaning efforts. "You don't have to help, Oliver."

Suitably chastised, Oli took the octopus from her clenched hand and settled it on one of the platforms of the nearest cat tree. "I'll just go stack some of these boxes out back, shall I?"

Pippa nodded, lips pressed tightly together as she watched him go.

"He's trying. I'm asking a lot from both of you to give this crazy idea a go," I said, wringing my hands together back and forth.

"Nonsense. It's a great idea. Exactly the solution we needed to solve our problems. And the cash injection from Mr. 999 didn't hurt either."

Heat rose in my cheeks, and I turned to busy myself rummaging through the box of tinned food and water bowls. "Officer Bardot is very generous indeed to support this business venture."

"Oh, it's *Officer Bardot*, is it?" Pippa asked. "Sounds kinky."

"It's not like that!" I snapped, standing up so quickly that I kicked the box halfway across the floor in haste. That did nothing to wipe the smirk off Pippa's lips. "We haven't done anything. At all. We haven't even had an official first date yet. Something always comes up."

Pippa's smile did slip then, softening into a knowing look. "Yeah, it's a real crime hotspot up here. Drug dealers, gang warfare, illicit nightlife. I imagine he's in the midst of it right now, sorting out a terrible case of cheating at the church's lunchtime bingo session."

"Ha ha," I said drily, turning back to the box and counting the bowls. "We did have a murder, you know. And that guy that was being held captive by his mother. It's not always boring up here in North Norfolk."

"Not always. But mostly," Pippa said. "That murder was a once-in-a-lifetime event. A total anomaly. The best you'll get for the next couple of decades is a turf war over a literal strip of turf between two neighbour's gardens."

"Maybe," I said. She was right. But I felt like defending my village of Catton Strawless as I had only moved here a few months ago, and my memories of it as a child were so rose-tinted that I considered it the best place in the world. But Pippa had grown up here her whole life, so she had far more experience on the happenings – or non-happenings – of the tiny village in rural North Norfolk.

As I bent to lay the dishes against a wall, assessing whether this was a good place for them not to be a trip hazard, the door to the café opened with the delightful jingle of the bell. We had opted to keep the café open during the refurb as much as possible.

"Good morning, how can I– oh, it's you," Pippa said, her sweet voice flattening as she identified our customer. "Willow, police. It's for you."

4

The blush returned to my cheeks as I sprang to my feet and then tried to meter my steps to not appear in a rush. "Officer, how can I help? Coffee?"

"Please," he said, watching me with strange rapt attention. "And a bacon roll."

"Uh," I began.

I didn't need to say the words. His face broke into a smile. "It's ok; I've got time to wait."

Bardot was familiar with our café's reputation. The best quality food in the East of England. Coupled with the slowest service time known to man. It was down to Pippa's insistence on using fresh ingredients and cooking to order. So, I dug bacon rashers from the fridge and set it frying while toasting a baguette and pouring him a large flat white.

"Busy day?" I asked.

"Yes. Prep work mainly, we've had an assignment come in. Top secret."

Upon hearing the word 'secret', Pippa was suddenly at the counter, elbows propping up her chin, ready to listen to the gossip.

"What part of 'top secret' don't you understand?" Bardot said.

"The part where I don't care, and you're going to tell us anyway. Otherwise, you wouldn't have mentioned it. So spill."

He heaved a sigh but stood up a little straighter as he began his story, clearly wanting to tell us as much as we wanted to hear it.

"It'll be in the local news this afternoon anyway. We have a distinguished guest arriving in Catton Strawless."

"Ooh, the king?" I asked, naming the poshest person I could think of. But then Sandringham estate was only a stone's throw away, so the King of England being here wasn't actually as big of a deal as it sounded.

"Not the king," Bardot said. "Georgie Weaver."

"Who?" I asked.

At the same time that Pippa gasped and clapped her hands to her mouth. "No. Way."

"Who is he?" I asked, my gaze snapping from Bardot to Pippa, searching for hints. "Actor? Rock band singer or something? Poet?"

"You haven't heard of Georgie Weaver?" Pippa asked, eagerly taking over the storytelling from a rather put-out-looking Bardot. "Did your aunt never tell you about him?"

I spent so much time in Catton Strawless in the summers when I was a child staying at my aunt's house. We had picnics in the park, picked wild strawberries and made sandcastles on the beach. But she'd never mentioned this man. I slowly shook my head.

Pippa sighed dramatically. "He was only the worst conman in Norfolk's history. He was a complete arse, did accounting for a lot of people around here, then stole a bunch of money and fled the country. And he lived right here, in the village. He lived a wonderful life in Spain or somewhere until he was finally arrested, and they locked him up and threw away the key."

"We don't actually throw away keys," Bardot felt the need to clarify.

"Wow, when was this?" I asked.

Pippa continued her story. "Late nineties. But he was only caught and brought back to the UK five years ago. I remember it being in the local news, and everyone in town was angry. Loads of people around here got scammed and lost a lot of money. And that's not the kind of thing they forget easily."

Bardot nodded thoughtfully. "Certainly, it will cause a stir."

"Why is he released now? He can't have done his time already?" Pippa asked.

"A judge has agreed to early release on compassionate grounds. He's terminally ill, not expected to live much longer."

"Pfft. Good riddance. I bet a lot of people around here will say the same. Why's he coming back? They repossessed his house, right? And he can't have any friends to bum a sofa from."

"His wishes were to return to the village he grew up in," Bardot shrugged. "He'll be staying at the Windmill Inn."

"So you're working out the security detail?" I guessed. "When the news breaks that he's coming here, it sounds like he's not going to get a friendly reception."

"Exactly. We're anticipating some mild unrest, but this is Catton Strawless, not the middle of London. I'm not expecting to need my old riot gear."

"I don't know, you haven't seen some of these old Norfolk boys when they're angry," I said. Pippa nodded fervently.

"I'm sure I'll manage, but thank you for the concern."

We fell into comfortable conversation, and Bardot had half finished his coffee by the time his bacon roll was ready. Once the café was fully refurbished, the aim was that customers would come for the experience, playing with and fussing over the cats while they waited for their order, which would hopefully keep complaints about the waiting time down.

"Good luck planning your crowd control," I called as Bardot left.

"Try not to tear gas too many pensioners," Pippa added.

As soon as the door closed, we burst into laughter.

"Rioting pensioners, classic," I said. "And you were just saying how dull it was around here."

Pippa wiped a tear from her eye. "Oh god, I needed that. Okay, my love, back to work. If we stick to the timeline, we'll need to get this stuff unpacked, and everything tidied away. We also need to get the rest of the painting done, not to mention designing the new menus and then adopt some cats. Can't open a cat café without cats."

"That would defeat the point," I agreed. "Leave that with me. I'm better with cats. I'll go to the shelters and find ones that will be happy to be around people. We don't want them stressed out; they need to be comfortable with noise and foot traffic."

Pippa nodded. "I'll get designing the menus. But I wanted to use the cats' names in them. Like Felix's Latte and Sock's Doughnuts."

"Do what you can, then we'll add the names once we have them," I suggested.

"Sounds great."

As I searched for shelter addresses, my news app pinged on my phone: **Dying Conman Released From Prison Early in Norfolk.**

And so it begins, I thought. Poor Bardot.

Two

Settling into my afterlife here on Earth has been easier than I thought. With the mystery of my death solved and my beloved human Eleanor's memory put to rest, I find myself quite content.

I also find myself drawn to other problems: principally my new human's love life. It's clear to me that she and the detective have a special something but he always seems so busy. We need something to force them to spend time together again.

It's almost a shame there isn't another case for them to work on.

--Thoughts from Luna

Again, Bardot had to cancel our coffee date as he was busy preparing for the prisoner to be escorted safely to the hotel. Bardot sent me tired texts as proof of life, but otherwise, the next three days for him were a mass of drills, staffing, meetings with the hotel and briefings to the media.

I spent the time painting murals on the walls of the café, helping Pippa and Oli with new menu items and phoning cat sanctuaries to find out what the cats were like and if they would be suitable for a café.

It was harder than I thought; many rescue cats were shy and unsuitable for such a large, noisy social environment. After explaining my plan for the fifth time that day to someone who didn't understand the business plan and, as it turned out, only had dogs, not cats, I gave up for the day and decided to stretch my legs.

The café wasn't busy, so I flipped the sign to closed and locked the door behind me.

"Good morning, Willow," said a passerby as I stepped onto the high street.

I wished them good morning, desperately searching for a name to go with the half-familiar face.

"Morning Willow," said another.

Again, no name came to mind, but I wished them a good day. Catton Strawless was a small village, isolated by its rurality, and everyone knew everyone. I was sure I'd start to know names soon enough.

They probably knew my name as I had recently risen to semi-fame as the solver of the only murder in the village in living memory.

A few weeks ago, my neighbour had been murdered by her ex-fiancé's mother, and my nosy interfering had actually solved the murder. I was pretty pleased with that, and it probably hadn't hurt my reputation.

Without realising it, my feet had taken me to the Windmill Inn. It was a beautiful three-story structure that could easily have been an eyesore but had been carefully built to keep with the village aesthetic. With homely flint walls and a tidy garden in shades of green with flowers bursting through the soil in explosions of colour, it blended well with the village despite its more recent construction.

Less natural, however, amidst the flower beds were people. Lots of people. Splashes of colour themselves, all facing the hotel front entrance and waving mobile phones high in the air to take pictures and videos.

"No photos!" yelled a lone police officer clad in a hi-visibility orange vest, his voice hoarse. "Please leave the area."

"This is public space, mate," yelled a middle-aged man with thinning grey hair.

"I'm staying until that murderer gets here, and then I'll give him what for," yelped a shrivelled older woman with her gnarled knuckles gripping the head of a walking stick.

It was then that I realised the colourful splashes were sleeping bags. Details of when Georgie would be arriving had been a guarded secret, but it seemed the public was angry enough to wait it out.

Cautiously I sidled up to the woman. "I heard he was a fraud and a conman; I didn't know he killed anyone"

"Not killed anyone?" she wailed. "Tell that to my son. My beautiful boy. He lost everything he did because of that animal. And then he killed himself from the shame. Right before his daughter was born, so he never met her. Poor little mite grew up without a father because of this maniac!"

Her voice rose to a shrill pitch that surely only dogs could hear but also drew the attention of several people setting up sophisticated camera rigging. The media were here, sleeping bags and thermal mugs emblazoned with the logos of their networks.

I could see their interest piqued; some were already fumbling for mics and handheld cameras to record the woman's story.

Realising that she had an audience, the hunch in her back became less pronounced as she straightened herself up to her full, unimpressive height and cleared her throat. Coincidentally this gave the media time to gather their kit and shove cameras in her face.

"It was 1999 that I first noticed the change in Freddie. It was the millennium, you see, so I remember it well. Y2K bugs and all that, it's all burned in my memory," she tapped a skeletal arthritic finger to her forehead.

"You mean Frederick Wainwright?" one of the cameramen asked. "The farm equipment entrepreneur?"

"One and the same," the woman said, seemingly happy to have her son's name recognised. "He lost six hundred and fifty thousand to that wretched waste of human flesh. All of his savings. Got into debt, more and more debt. By the time he realised everything had gone wrong, he was in too deep, owed thousands, and faced losing his home. He couldn't live with himself and the trust he had put in his accountant. He finally took his own life when the sleazeball fled and couldn't be found, and Freddie knew there was no way to get his money back."

"And the child?" one woman asked, pushing the mic closer to hear the little catch in the woman's throat.

"Oh yes, that poor little girl. She was born after he died and never knew him. But the anger burns deep. She blames Georgie Weaver for what he did to her father. She'll never forget."

Never forget.

Those words were etched into the faces of the dozens gathered here. Whether they had lost directly or their family had been affected, it seemed Georgie Weaver had left a poisonous legacy here in Catton Strawless. Why on earth did he want to return here for his final days? To find peace? He wasn't going to get that here, with protestors camped outside his hotel and ready to stay and hurl abuse at him for the long haul.

Bardot had his work cut out for him protecting Georgie.

That night, spurred on by a glass of wine, I sifted through some old boxes of my aunt's old paperwork. They were box files overstuffed with various papers – bank and mortgage statements, medical letters, receipts, and bills with the date paid neatly printed in biro. My aunt kept everything.

I had been meaning to find a way to get rid of it all – as she was dead and the accounts were closed, did I need to shred them? – but hadn't got around to it. I'd shoved them in the spare room and largely forgotten about them since inheriting the house. My time had been taken up by a murder investigation and planning for the cat café.

But as my movie night with Bardot had been cancelled, I had a free evening.

"Mow?" a cool nose nudged my hand, and bright blue eyes watched me curiously from a frame of fluffy white fur.

"Luna, how are you doing?" I asked, running my hands through her silky pelt.

"Mow," she trilled, dipping her back into a yoga pose and stretching her paws out as she closed her eyes in bliss.

"I'm just looking through some old papers. Be careful; the staples are a bit rusty." I cautioned though Luna was happy enough to stay put and let me scratch behind her ears with one hand, the other leafing through documents.

"So much paper for one life," I mumbled to nobody in particular. "It was all important once."

I sighed and drew my hand back from the piles. What was I looking for, really? What had sparked me to start searching through them now, tonight? What had stirred these ghosts in my mind?

"Mow." Luna sprang to her feet, shaking her pelt free of my hand and padding over to them.

"Staples," I warned in a low voice.

She sniffed the sheets of paper, her whiskers gently tickling them as her nose twitched. Then she gripped an A4 white envelope with her teeth and dragged it out of the pile.

"Found something you like?" I asked, picking it up. "It doesn't have any treats in it, you know?"

"Mow," she explained.

"Okay, I'll look." The envelope was slightly dogeared from age, and there was no address. It had never been posted. But in the same neat hand that had dated the bills was a set of initials in the corner: GW.

"No way. Not Georgie Weaver?" I asked myself.

"Mow," Luna purred sagely.

Hurriedly I tipped out the contents of the thick envelope onto the bed in front of me. There were yellowed newspaper clippings, the back and white mugshot of a man slightly balding but with a thick beard and a smirk on his lips that showed no remorse at being finally caught.

"Why did Aunt Dawn have these?" I asked myself.

Deep down, I knew the answer.

There were dozens of news articles that chronicled the discovery of Georgie's crime, through to the discovery he had fled the country and finally to his capture and extradition to the UK and sentencing. My aunt had kept every scrap of news about him.

Underneath them were printed documents. Copies of bank statements with lines picked out in now-faded yellow highlighter. Thick creamy paper with a gold-embossed logo of a solicitors firm. My aunt had sought legal advice for the sum of seven thousand pounds she lost when her accountant stole it from her account.

"Oh, Auntie Dawn..." I breathed softly, sitting back on my heels with the papers fanned around me. A historical account of how she had been scammed by someone she had trusted.

Now I felt a kindred link with those camping outside the hotel. A flame of anger ignited within me, a growing desire to see him pay. How could he be released early? Did he deserve to die a free man when so many people he hurt had died shackled by the effects of the fraud?

My hands trembled as I forced myself to read the newspaper articles from start to finish. Then the letters to and from the solicitors, ending with a final note apologising that the money was irretrievable.

How many people camped outside the hotel had similar letters in a keepsake box somewhere? A toxic memento of a past they would love to bury but couldn't as they were still feeling the effects.

My aunt lost seven thousand pounds. Of course, others had lost more, Frederick Wainwright the most. But that seven grand was important to her.

"Mow?" Luna nudged my hip with her head, a surefire sign that she felt she was overdue a treat.

Gathering the papers, I put them back in their envelope and at the bottom of a box file. Perhaps if I buried them deep the anger I felt toward this man would fade faster.

"Come on then, Luna. Let's get you a treat. You deserve it for finding that envelope."

Although I still wasn't sure if I was happier in the knowledge or if ignorance had been bliss.

Because now I burned with a desire to commit a murder of my own.

Three

Now my human is sad again. That happens when she thinks of her special person – Aunt Dawn. Willow rarely mentions her parents but from what I can gather her fondest memories are of weekends and summer holidays spent here with her aunt.

To find that her aunt had been tricked of money seems to have hurt Willow. The way her hands balled into fists and her eyes narrowed. Classic cat signs of discontent.

--Thoughts from Luna

I knew the exact moment that Georgie Weaver arrived in Catton Strawless.

Not through some mystical sixth sense or anything. I could hear the crowd jeering, even from my tiny house several streets away from the hotel, tucked up in bed as I was.

"Huhn?" I blearily asked the alarm clock, which cheerfully blinked back the time at me. 6:45.

"Too early," I mumbled, turning over in bed only to find myself face to face with a pair of intense and hungry green eyes.

"Mrow," Loki said.

"Seriously?"

"Mrow."

"Ok then, I guess it's not too early."

Twenty minutes later, I was showered, dressed and pouring some PsyTreats into bowls for Loki and Luna. These are little crunchy biscuits made with a standard cat treat recipe I found online, but with a little extra magic that only I can add to the mix, which enables ghost cats to eat them and feel a psychic energy boost that is one part energy drink, one part warm hug. The cats love them.

My shoulder-length blonde hair was still damp, but the fact that I could still hear commotion had woken me up far faster than hungry cats could.

"He's coming then," I said to nobody in particular since the cats were more interested in crunching their food than a dying criminal.

The sky was slate grey, the clouds stiflingly low as if trying to press us down into the earth. The air was heavy with a sense of anticipation and probably the coming of a storm. Whether meteorological or human was yet to be seen.

Leaving the house, I made my way to the café taking the scenic route by the Windmill Inn. It was still very early, but everyone who had camped outside was wide awake and loudly voicing their dissent. Tents flapped in the wind, and I marvelled at how quickly word had spread.

The police presence had increased. Now four officers stood like statues with their hands clasped behind their backs, staring at nothing. Orange traffic cones sat in a car-shaped spot in front of the grand hotel doors, assumedly ready for the transport vehicle to drop Georgie off in privacy.

Good luck with privacy: there were dozens of people, dishevelled from waking suddenly, holding phones to record. The media had large cameras mounted on stands and microphones wrapped in wind muffs hung expectantly, ready to capture every moment.

"Not long now, then?" I asked a man my age, who was wearing pyjamas and had just crawled out of his tent.

"No, Peter heard about it first. He's got a radio set to the police channels. He heard that the transport was on its way from the prison. Weaver will be here any second. Got my fruit ready."

"Fruit?" I asked, momentarily confused as to why he would be so concerned about his five a day at a time like this.

I understood when he held up a crate of rotting strawberries, pears and mangoes.

"Found these beauties in the stock room at work, someone forgot to clear out. My lucky day, right?"

"Yes, well done," I said, suddenly unsure that I wanted to stand so close in case I got arrested alongside him.

As more people joined the gathering, the crowd swelled and pressed close. Warm bodies shoved against me, and placards rose into the air, each jostling to get in front of the media cameras to have their five seconds in the spotlight.

Suddenly I didn't want to be there. What was I playing at? I should squeeze my way out of the crowd and go to work or for a long walk to clear my head. I had no business heckling an elderly, frail, dying man in his final days when all he wanted was to be in his childhood village to die.

Shame burned within me as I turned to leave, but that was easier said than done. I nearly tripped over wires from lighting rigging, trod on the tail of a rottweiler and apologised profusely to an equally snappy owner, then got elbowed in the boob by a woman who was flailing about shrieking her head off about reinstating the death penalty.

So slow was my progress that it was soon too late to leave.

The crowd fell so silent it was as if time stood still. The rumble of the approaching vehicle and the flutter of banners was all I could hear as the crowd collectively held its breath. Since I was here anyway, I pushed closer to the front, peeking between bodies as I stared down the street and watched the white, blue and yellow police van approach.

And then, as if a dam had burst, the noise exploded again.

Screaming. Shrieking. Stomping feet. From the second the car rolled to a stop directly outside the hotel doors, the crowd's roar was deafening. Ashamedly, I joined it. I told myself it was to fit in; if I joined in, the public wouldn't turn on me. I would be one of them.

Or had I gone native?

When the van doors opened, I didn't even notice Bardot. My gaze narrowed on the figure of Georgie Weaver, and suddenly the screams from my lips were no longer just for show. The abuse I hurled was real, raw and guttural. It was for Auntie

Dawn, who couldn't express her anger, frustration and shame at being lied to by this hideous excuse for a man.

Rotten fruit pelted the side of the car. Georgie was on the far side and already being ushered inside, so nothing hit him, unfortunately. Part of me was tempted to grab a handful of strawberries and shove the rotten fruit up Georgie's nose.

Georgie paused at the door and turned to the crowd. Bardot was at his side, urging him on, but Georgie couldn't help himself. He turned and blew the crowd a kiss as if we were his adoring fans and he was gifting us with his presence.

Boos erupted all around me, and I delighted in joining in.

Georgie wasn't the frail, older man I'd thought he was. He couldn't have been more than his late fifties, and his full-framed body was dressed in a branded white tracksuit. His hair retained a rusty hint of its youthful red, and his beard was as thick and full as ever.

"Thank you, thank you," Georgie called, his voice strong, carrying even over the booing.

Then he stuck two fingers up on each hand at us, cackled manically and ducked into the hotel.

The crowd surged forward, and I was swept up as if caught in a current. The booing morphed into howling. The poor four police officers desperately tried to keep everyone out, but in the end, a few people managed to storm the lobby and take up their rioting inside. Georgie was long gone, travelling in the lift to who knew which room.

Finally, I managed to break free by ducking between people and dodging elbows, feet and the general surge of the crowd. I popped out the other side into the fresh, crisp air and sucked in several lungfuls, glad to be away from the press of bodies.

With the echoes of angry yelling ringing in my ears, I hurried away, hoping that the fury within me would fade the further I got from the peer pressure of others. Distantly I heard Sergeant Campbell trying – and failing – to calm the crowd.

Business was booming.

We had planned to scale back the café operations while we were refurbishing, but with the media camped out in our little village and people coming far and wide to hurl profanities at Georgie Weaver, the few cafés in Catton Strawless were packed. That antisocial behaviour was thirsty work, after all.

There were a few grumbles about how long it took us to make the freshly prepared food, but once they took a bite, their frowns melted like the cheese in our breakfast bap. Besides, it wasn't like they were flush with choices for a hot snack within walking distance. The joys of rural living; less competition.

The refurb itself was put on the back burner while we hurried about fulfilling orders and restocking to meet the demand. I didn't even think about adopting cats for nearly two weeks until the crowds started to disperse as the interest died away. Georgie never left his hotel room. None of the plucky vandals had managed to scale the building or enter from the hall. It was generally accepted that there was no way to get to him and that he wasn't going to die immediately, so interest waned.

However, one customer you could count on like clockwork was a tall, lanky youth with close-cropped brown hair and glasses that always looked slightly askew as if they'd been broken and poorly repaired. He hurried in all senses of the word: his actions, speech, even when he unlocked his phone to swipe a payment, his hands were shaking with the need for haste. Isaac was a sweet boy and personal nurse to Georgie Weaver. Perhaps that's why he always looked like a startled owl.

This morning he bounced on the balls of his feet while he waited behind a mum doing the school rush, then hopped up to the counter and leaned close.

"Double espresso and bacon melt to go, please." Except it was pronounced all as one word.

"Coming right up," I flashed a smile at him.

He wore his pale blue nursing tunic over black trousers and scuffed brown shoes. He kept glancing at the cheap plastic watch on his wrist while I filled his order.

"How is he today?" I asked casually. Hoping my voice didn't betray my real question, *'is he going to die anytime soon?'*

"Oh, you know, same old," Isaac muttered, shyly addressing his feet instead of me. "Always more pain in the mornings and at night. Gave him his morphine and cup of tea, so he's perking up a bit. He's watching Deal Quest on telly and told me to bugger off, so here I am."

"Charming."

"He's...yeah. He pays well," Isaac said as if that was the most positive thing he could say about his employer.

"So what do you do when you're 'buggering off', then?" I asked, popping a lid on his takeout coffee.

"You know, here and there. Odd jobs. Pharmacy a lot, picking up various meds and stuff. He needs bandages changing, he had a stroke a while ago which left him incontinent, so I have to get pads...oh god, I shouldn't be telling you any of this! I'm so sorry."

Chuckling, I handed him the bacon melt wrapped in wax paper. I winked at him, which caused him to blush to the roots of his hair. Then I mimed zipping my mouth closed. "I won't tell a soul."

"Th-thanks. I have to go otherwise, Chloe...the pharmacy..."

I nodded wisely. "You need to get to the pharmacy while Chloe is still on shift? Well, I promise to keep that gossip between us too."

If possible, his blush deepened further. How he didn't spontaneously combust, I have no idea. I was slightly concerned he was about to overheat and pass out, but he stuttered out a few words that might have been thanks or could equally have been an impression of a squeaky mouse toy, then darted out of the door. Pushing instead of pulling and almost breaking his glasses anew when he headbutted the door.

"Bye," I called when he finally navigated the exit.

"Interesting," I said, drumming my fingertips on the glass worktop.

"What is?" Pippa asked, entering the café floor from the back office.

"Isaac. Georgie's nurse. Lovely kid, what the hell he's doing working for Georgie, I don't know."

Pippa shrugged. "Money? He's so young. Maybe it was hard to get a nursing job when he's just qualified. Hell, maybe he's Georgie's grandson for all we know. Does it matter?"

"No. Yes. No. I just wonder. With our nursing shortages, you'd think he'd have been snapped up. What's a kid like him doing out here in the middle of nowhere?"

Pippa nudged me with her elbow. "Hey, enough of that. We're hardly over the hill, and we choose to live in the backend of nowhere. It's charming."

"It is," I agreed. But there was something more. Something about Isaac that I couldn't put my finger on.

Four

Not sure what the humans are so worked up about. I took a snoop around the hotel room the old human is staying in, it's nothing special.

It smells a bit sterile but also of toast. The television is constantly on game shows and antiques programmes, turned up to a volume that must disturb the neighbours. I approve.

The old human himself spends most of his time sitting up in bed, on the armchair, or by the window. Just watching. He revels in antagonising people.

Especially his nurse, a human who resembles a giraffe in stature and build but has the meekness of a mouse.

--Thoughts from Loki

Sunday afternoon, on my way back from grocery shopping at the big Tesco out of town, a police car zipped past. Its siren blared, and lights flashed as it screeched around a corner and then out of sight. Heading toward Catton Strawless.

Now I didn't need to be a genius to work out what could have caused that.

Curiosity killed the cat, but I wasn't a cat, so I'd be fine, right?

Hoping my shopping would survive a quick peek, I followed the police car into the village and up to the Windmill Inn. I parked a hundred metres away and power walked to the front of the hotel, where the police car had parked at an angle. Two officers had jumped out and were struggling to get the situation under control.

"Everybody back away," called a tall officer wearing aviator sunglasses. "Please leave the area if you have no business being here."

"I have every business being here. That thief stole my inheritance!" yelled the fruit thrower from the first day Georgie arrived.

"When I say business, I mean that you are staying at the hotel. If not, please disperse," aviator glasses said.

The wizened older woman stood her ground. "I've pitched my tent here, so technically, I'm staying at the hotel."

"You have *illegally* pitched your tent," the police officer began but was interrupted by the woman who stormed up to him and jabbed a bony finger at his chest.

"And he *illegally* took my son's money. Which is worse, huh? Stealing or putting a tent on a bit of grass? Answer me that!" A finger jab punctuated every word.

Aviator glasses was losing control of the situation, and the younger officer he had brought with him had already tried to melt into the background, not wanting to confront the angry mob.

"Let 'em stay. I don't have much amusement in my life," called a voice, drifting down as if from the heavens.

Of course, it wasn't some divine intervention. It was Georgie Weaver, leaning comfortably out of his hotel room window and watching the people gathered below as if he were a lord in his high tower.

"Please sir, close your window and move further inside," called aviator glasses.

"No thanks, sonny. Spent enough of my days locked away."

Aviator Glasses was paralysed by confusion as to whether to continue his futile attempts at crowd control or divert all his efforts to persuade Georgie to leave the window. He was saved the decision by his young colleague, who hurried up to him and said something I couldn't hear.

Aviator glasses nodded. "Everybody, please go home. I have official business to attend to, and you are wasting police time."

The officers snapped on their heels and scurried into the hotel like cats spooked by a firework. Beaten by the crowd but trying to retain dignity and an illusion that they had somehow won. The hecklers returned to their fold-up chairs or retreated to their tents to recharge for the next round.

Intrigued and unable to help myself, I casually made my way to the hotel and slipped inside, the warmth and sweet scent of the lobby enveloping me as I passed through the thick glass doors.

Cautiously I crossed the marble floor, conscious that my footsteps echoed loudly and I didn't want to attract attention.

The marble was polished to a glassy finish, and I had to suppress a giggle picturing Loki trying to make his way across and ice skating on his paws as he failed to find a grip.

The lobby was tall and spacious, the pale marble of the floor offset by dark grey walls with gold trim. A golden staircase wound up to the upper floors, and two lifts were next to the heavy dark wooden reception desk.

I found an area of armchairs and low coffee tables and sat down, pretending to flip through one of the complimentary glossy magazines while eavesdropping on the conversation between the police and the receptionist.

"So where is he now?" asked aviator glasses.

"Outside Mr Weaver's suite, in the hallway. He refuses to budge, and the officer at the door can't persuade him to leave and has requested assistance for an arrest," said the receptionist, a small man wearing the back and white uniform of the hotel, which conjured the unfortunate image of a penguin.

"We'll go talk to him," the policeman promised with a reassuring air of authority he had lacked when dealing with the crowd outside.

The officers were gone with a ping of the lift doors. While I waited, I read an article about Tenerife and planned a wonderful sun-drenched beach holiday in my head. I was spirited away to a vineyard and sipping an imaginary glass of sweet chilled white wine when the lift doors pinged again, opening so that the raised voices spilt into the lobby.

"–know my rights. You can't arrest me. I wasn't doing anything wrong!" boomed a voice so abruptly and loudly that I almost dropped the magazine in fright.

Slowly I lowered the magazine so I could glimpse the man that the police had come to arrest. He was a mountain of muscle, a black shirt straining against his biceps, his neck thick, his head shaved in a buzzcut. His hands clenched into fists, and I didn't doubt his ability to use them.

The two police officers – a good head shorter than the man – were trying to enact some semblance of authority.

"Disturbing the peace," the younger officer squeaked.

"Peace? What peace?" the man spat. "With that lot out there on the grass, you think me being in a hotel hallway is disturbing anything? You're having a laugh."

"Please come with us?" aviator glasses said, though it sounded more like a question than an order. His sunglasses were perched on top of his head now. Whether it was an attempt to look cool or they were more of a hindrance inside, it was hard to tell. He certainly didn't look cool. In fact, he looked flustered, and without the glasses I could see a spark of fear in his eyes.

"Don't think I will, but nice try," the man said, pushing past them both and leaning across the reception desk. "Get a message to Georgie. Tell him The Jawbreaker is out of prison and ready to collect his payment. I'm not looking for trouble, just ready to get what's rightfully mine, you see? Georgie will want to speak to me; we're old jailbird friends. And we have unfinished business."

"Y-yes, sir," the receptionist gasped, sounding more likely to faint than pass on a message.

"Any problems?" the man – Jawbreaker? – asked the two police.

They seemed disinclined to continue their attempt at arresting him.

Jawbreaker grinned and snapped a salute at them. "I'll be back tonight. And I expect to speak to Georgie and get my money."

The lobby was blanketed in silence, so I heard every thump of Jawbreaker's footsteps as he left. And the collective sigh of the police and receptionist once the doors swung closed.

"What do we do?" asked the younger police.

"We never mention it again. He's not wrong. He wasn't technically breaking the law if he wanted to speak to an old friend. So that's what we'll write in the report. Got it?"

"Yessir."

Once they had gone, I lowered the magazine and replaced it on the stack. Curious and curiouser. It seemed Georgie Weaver left trails all over the place. What on earth could Jawbreaker have done in prison that warranted Georgie paying him?

And I shuddered to think how someone earned the nickname "Jawbreaker".

I took my slightly defrosted shopping home to unpack, then took a few moments to set out some PsyTreats for the cats before settling down for the evening on the sofa with a cup of coffee and some microwaved lasagne to do some research. Not that I particularly had a goal in mind, but my ever-present sense of curiosity and need to know were kicking in.

Loading a new browser window, I typed in "Jawbreaker". And, of course, I was presented with a list of websites offering to sell me brightly coloured retro sweets. In the interest of my dental bill, I retried the search with a few more parameters.

Bingo. *The* Jawbreaker, not just Jawbreaker. Originally he came from London and had been in trouble with the law a few times over street fights and being drunk and disorderly. He had owned a wrestling ring with his brother until they fell out over money, and he beat the brother senseless, seriously breaking his jaw. Hence the nickname.

Once released on parole, he had started afresh and set up a new gym. Again a string of minor arrests and infarctions followed him until he once again fell out with his business partner and this time bashed his head in with a chair. There was a whole news article on the incident, another on his incarceration at Norwich prison, and finally, his release about three weeks ago.

Apparently he had fallen in love with Norfolk and decided to stay. Presumably to set up another gym so that he could attempt to murder another business partner.

I also learned that The Jawbreaker's real name was Ricky Moreno.

"Huh," I said, closing my laptop and draining the last inch of my coffee. Curiosity satisfied, I felt myself silently rooting for Ricky. If he could cause a little grief and make Georgie pay a debt, then at least that would give Georgie a taste of the fear his victims had felt. But it did leave a bad taste in my mouth that I was in any way sympathetic to an alcoholic criminal who thrived on beating people bloody.

What a strange world we lived in.

Sensing my inner turmoil, Luna jumped onto my lap and curled into a little snowy ball, purring softly like a little motor. My fingers lazily scratched her coat's long fur, and she melted against me in pure bliss.

Lulled by her vibration, the warm coffee inside me and the fact I had nothing pressing to do, I found myself drifting off, curled up safe on the sofa.

Once again, I was woken early. This time by sirens.

Five

I do not enjoy being woken up prematurely. I wake up when I choose to wake up and not a whisker before.

This had better be good.

--Thoughts from Loki

"Hiiiiisss." Loki's back arched in a fury, having also been startled awake from his dreams.

Luna was more dignified about it, sitting up and licking her paws as if she had meant to wake up all along.

My reaction was somewhere between the two, grumpy that I had been startled awake but curious about the source of the commotion. My phone blinked up the time at me: 6:36. Too damn early o'clock.

Reaching my arms up into a stretch, my shoulders popped, and my back creaked, but the little clicks felt damn good. Sleeping on the sofa is not healthy for your posture. And leaving your dirty lasagne plate on the coffee table overnight makes for an unhappy dishwasher. The neon orange sauce looked like it wouldn't budge for anything less than industrial intervention.

As I extracted myself from the sofa and carried the mess to the kitchen, I briefly weighed the pros and cons of paper plates until another siren cut through the air. I almost dropped the dish (at least I'd have been free of the task of cleaning it).

"Mrow!" Loki snapped. For a cat, he was horribly grouchy in the morning, especially when he hadn't woken up on his own terms.

"Growling at the sirens won't make them stop," I advised him, but that didn't stop his grumble of discontent as he tried to curl up and bury his head under his paws.

I dressed quickly and was out of the door into the first rays of morning light. The air was fresh and clear, amplifying the sirens as the wails carried across the village. As I passed houses, I could see lights on, curtains drawn, and even people popping heads out of doors and windows.

"Whatever now?" asked a woman wrapped tight in her dressing gown, standing on her dew-dampened lawn in a pair of fluffy beige slippers.

"No idea, but I imagine it involves our esteemed guest," I said as I hurried past.

"Pah," the woman spat and decided it wasn't worth getting her slippers wet. She disappeared back inside with a slam that rattled the glass in her door

The sirens had ceased, but my feet knew where to go. The hotel was bathed in a pink dawn light as the sky awoke in a palette of magenta and orange. The grass dampened my feet as I joined those who had left their tents to investigate.

To my surprise, while there were two police cars, there was also an ambulance.

"What's going on?" I asked the fruit thrower from my first day stalking the hotel.

"Not a clue, love," he said. The venom had faded from his voice, softening it into confusion and concern. Nobody can see an ambulance and not feel a little well of compassion deep within themselves.

"Do you think it's even Georgie?" I asked.

The sudden realisation hit me that a guest could have had an accident or died overnight and that Georgie Weaver staying here was just a coincidence. Guilt pricked at me to be standing here gawking without knowing the facts. I was two seconds from turning away and leaving when the wizened old lady spoke up.

"No, the light went on in Georgie's room like usual for his early morning meds. Morphine for the pain and blood thinners he has. Then the light goes off, and half an hour later, he has his breakfast – two rounds of buttered toast, slices of Galia melon and a bowl of porridge. With maple syrup and raisins."

How the hell she knew that I didn't want to know. Fruit Thrower and I paused to let her continue as to what conclusion she had drawn from this.

"His light went on at six thirty like it always does, then never went out." She nodded her head sagely. "Something's up. Mark my words."

"Do you think he died?" I asked, a shiver running through my body that had nothing to do with the early morning chill. "He did get released early because he was so ill."

"That old goat?" Fruit Thrower laughed. "I'm sure he was scamming the parole board just like he scammed our village."

"Mmm," I hummed softly, not wanting to get into a discussion about how someone could go about faking terminal cancer.

Once again, I was ready to go. The morning was still, the protestors seemingly confused about what to do, and my tits were cold as ice. As soon as I'd decided to leave, however, the doors to the hotel opened. Detective Constable Bardot emerged. Radiating no-nonsense confidence, he strode up to those gathered on the grass.

"Good morning. I need everyone here to follow me into the hotel. We have the conference room booked, and I will need to take names and statements from everyone who was out here last night. If anyone has since left, and you have their details or even a description, that would be very helpful. Thank you."

"What's going on?" asked a tall, rail-thin man with a comically large moustache.

"As you can see, there has been an incident. We just need a statement and details from you at this stage, and then you will be free to go. And I strongly suggest you leave, take your tents and move on."

The finality in his voice stopped any argument, and people queued and shuffled through the doors to make their statements.

I glanced at my phone and saw it was still too early to go to the café, so I slipped in after them. After all, I'd technically been there, even if it was after the incident had happened, so I felt my presence semi-validated.

Also, they had a table of coffee and pastries set out.

I poured myself a cup and took a flaky croissant, then perched myself on a velvet chair closest to where an officer was sitting at a circular table with a laptop and phone for recording and was interviewing each person in turn.

"Name?" the officer asked.

"Jamie Robinson," said the fruit thrower.

A few more boring personal details told me Jamie was a few years younger than me, lived in Mundesley but had travelled here when he heard Georgie was arriving. He had felt compelled to protest as his family had been robbed of their life savings, gone into debt and sold the family home. Jamie had been left with no inheritance. The police officer seemed unmoved by Jamie's plight.

"He's dead, isn't he?" Jamie interrupted the first question.

"I'm sorry, sir, I can't–"

"He is. You wouldn't be doing this if he wasn't. Well, I hope it was painful. I hope he suffered."

"Sir, if we could just–"

"There's tonnes like me, you know?" Jamie leaned over the table slightly, a sneer on his lips. "People he shafted. People who hold a grudge. Maybe he was really dying, and maybe he wasn't. But if I were you, I'd take a second look at the body because, with this many enemies, his death may not have been as natural as you think."

The police officer's mouth snapped shut. He tapped his fingers on the edge of the table and considered Jamie for so long that the smug smirk dropped from Jamie's lips, and he started to look a little nervous.

"Sorry, what was the question again?" Jamie muttered.

"It's fine, sonny," the police officer said. His voice was softer, more understanding. He no longer pushed his questions. Instead, he waved over Bardot. "This is Detective Constable Bardot. I think it would be worthwhile for you to have a private chat with him in one of the spare rooms."

Bardot nodded as if a secret code had been slipped to him. He heaved Jamie to his feet and marched him off without even a word.

Jamie panicked, his feet barely dusting the floor as he was hauled off for further questioning.

"No, no, I was joking! Joking! What are you doing? Get off me!"

A white-painted wooden door bearing a bronze "staff only" plaque closed sharply behind them, cutting off Jamie's complaints and leaving the conference hall in silence for a long, uncomfortable moment.

"Next, please," the police officer said sweetly.

I didn't stick around for a second coffee. I did steal a cinnamon whirl to eat on the go.

Licking icing from my fingertips, I stuck my key in the lock of the café but found it was already open. My heart skipped a beat as I panicked it had been unlocked all night, but when I stepped into the warmth, a wave of coffee scent washed over me, and Pippa's face smiled from over the counter.

"Morning darling," she called.

"Morning. Did the sirens wake you up too?"

"Couldn't not, could it?" she said, sipping from a mug of what I guessed was tea. "I assume you went straight there?"

My cheeks heated under her knowing gaze. "Am I that obvious?"

"Yes. But that's ok. You may be nosy as sin, but you get the good gossip. So spill, what's happening? Did the old crook pop his clogs or what?"

"I'm pretty sure. There was an ambulance there, and two police cars, and then Bardot came out and was like all, 'you all have to come inside and give statements' then they hauled this guy away into another room for further interrogation and–"

"Whoa whoa whoa, slow you down." Pippa hurried around the counter and dragged a chair to sit at a table. "Sit. Start from the start."

I sat. I started from the start. "I got there, and all the campers were pretty confused. The ambulance and police just turned up, nobody even knew why, but they assumed it was Georgie."

I explained what had happened, and Pippa encouraged me whenever I paused slightly too long to draw breath.

"So that's it, he's dead?" Pippa said when I'd finally finished. "He was dying anyway. That's why they let him out, right? Not sure why it needed such a song and dance."

"See, that's the thing, I think he's dead. But I don't think it was natural. When I overheard Jamie being interviewed, the police officer completely changed when he joked about murder. Like he had hit the nail on the head."

"Oooh, you think murder is afoot?" Pippa said, then her face scrunched into a frown. "But why? Why bother with the risk of murdering a dying man? He'll be dead soon anyway, and the would-be murderer doesn't have to worry about being caught."

"Cancer is too impersonal. Whoever killed Georgie Weaver wanted him to know about it, I think. They wanted Georgie to see them, to know they were prematurely taking his life as revenge for what he did."

Pippa let out a low whistle and leaned back in her chair. "Jeez. That narrows the suspect list to…oh, maybe a couple hundred? If you consider the victims themselves and any family affected by it."

"Yes, but there'll be some that took it better, some who didn't know he was released, and some that weren't here last night. The number of campers has gone down. There's only a dozen or so still there anymore."

"Let's face it if you were going to commit murder, why would you make it so obvious that you camp out in front of your victim? It's like painting a target on your forehead."

"Exactly what I was thinking. And Jamie went ghost-white when the police accused him of murder. They were angry, yes. But I don't think anyone on the grass killed Georgie. The police need to be looking for someone with a grudge rooted so deep that they couldn't even stand to be that close to Georgie."

I paused, thinking.

"Or, you know, they just have a job and couldn't camp out for a week."

"Or that," Pippa agreed. "Speaking of jobs, shall we open up to our adoring public? Murder or not, if Georgie is dead, the media vans will be piling in again, and that's more hungry and thirsty customers. I might need to do a run to get more stock."

And so began yet another busy day.

If only I knew then what was to come.

Six

Hm. Begrudgingly I have to admit that it was something good. I suppose being awoken so rudely was worth it.

Of course I had a nose around, why not? Nobody could see me. Luna didn't want to come, said it reminded her too much of her own death which is still raw. But I fancied a look.

The old human appeared to be sleeping. He seemed perfectly peaceful, tucked up in bed. Bit of drool on the pillow, hair a mess and one arm sticking out from under the covers.

Nothing abnormal but the room was a bit messy. Some trash on the floor, glass of some kind. But nothing amiss particularly. Another human popping off his mortal coil.

--Thoughts from Loki

It was mid-morning when the media cavalry arrived en mass, the lone reporters still stationed there having called for backup at the first hint of a story.

The local newspaper got the first pictures, but the regional and then national crews weren't far behind. By eleven o'clock, every inch of space outside the hotel had been claimed by cameras, vans and people speaking excitedly on phones.

I knew because I was back and forth from the café delivering hot beverages and late breakfasts to the dozens of journalists and photographers who couldn't possibly spare a moment to visit the café in person in case they missed any action.

Every time I returned to the café for more stock Pippa grilled me on what was happening.

"Have they taken his body out yet?"

"Are there forensic units?"

"Is the Daily World there?"

"Has Bardot made a statement yet?"

"Are we definitely sure it's Georgie and not another guest or something?"

I had very few answers to any of that, although during my last trip, a police forensic van had finally arrived, and three people in floofy white overalls piled out with boxes of equipment.

Which fuelled my theory that the police suspected Georgie hadn't died naturally.

My feet burned with a deep ache in the arches, and I longed to kick off my shoes and give them a good rub, but when I finally finished my trips back and forth, I returned to The Mews and Beans Cat Café to find Pippa with yet another order packed for me.

"You're kidding me!" I groaned, sinking into a chair. "No more. Please, no more."

"Oh, I think you'll want to do this one," Pippa said with a smile, popping the paper bag and coffee on the table and turning it so I could see the name printed on the bag.

I brightened up instantly, like a dried-up flower sprinkled with water. "Oh, alright then, I suppose I have one more trip in me."

"Bring back the goss," Pippa called after me.

As if I needed reminding.

This time I strode confidently through the crowd, careful not to knock over cameras, step on picnics or bash my head on a dead cat microphone. I carried the little paper bag and cup without spilling a drop to the hotel doors, where two police officers stopped me.

"Business?" one asked.

I held up the bag with its name clearly printed. "Delivery."

They nodded me through, and the glass doors snapped shut behind me, completely cutting silent the din of the media frenzy outside. I hadn't realised how loud all those voices had been until I was in the strange, echoing silence of the lobby.

A few slow steps in, my heels echoing on the marble, I realised I was alone. The reception desk was empty, nobody sat on the comfortable armchairs browsing a magazine, and the lifts were silent, fixed at whatever floor they had been summoned to.

Part of me expected an axe murderer to leap out at any second and carve me up into bloody pieces that he would dispose of, perhaps in weighted fishing netting in a deep lake.

Another part of me recognised how unrealistic and oddly specific my fear was. And also that it was the plot of a recent episode of Crime Busters I had watched.

"Willow?"

"Aargh!" I screamed, nearly dropping the coffee. I anticipated an axe burying into my back any second.

"What's wrong?" Bardot asked urgently, running to meet me.

"N-nothing. Sorry. Just thought you were a murderer." Heat raced up my cheeks, and I hurriedly handed him the bag. "I brought your breakfast. Brunch. Lunch?"

For a second, his mouth hung open as if he wanted to comment on the fact I had leapt to the conclusion that he was a murderer, and then he shook his head clear of the thought and took the bag and the coffee. "Thanks."

"Speaking of murderers, how is your day going?" I asked.

"Subtle. Real subtle," he said, gulping his coffee and looking as if he could use an IV drip of it.

"Anything you can tell me? You know I'm good at this stuff. I solved your last murder."

His eyebrows raised, but he was spared snorting with laughter as he was taking another deep drink of coffee. I was lucky I didn't end up wearing it. "You got yourself kidnapped and almost killed."

"I identified the murderer and found the son she was holding hostage. Credit where credit is due."

"Hnn," he grunted, sounding a bit like a wild pig.

"I know it was a murder. One of the officers took away a witness this morning when he joked about murder. And I'm sure I saw the crime scene techs arrive. And you wouldn't be doing all this if Georgie had died in his sleep of cancer."

"Who says Georgie is dead?"

"The entire village and the national media stations."

"Hnn," he grumbled again.

"So is that the official response then? 'Hnn'?" I asked, attempting the nasal sound myself.

Ever the perfect cop, Bardot glanced around the empty lobby. But then I had thought it was empty before, and he'd sneaked up on me, so maybe a second pair of trained eyes was helpful.

"Yes, Georgie Weaver died last night."

"I knew it!" I said, then realised I was getting excited over someone dying, and shame burned within me. Then I remembered who it was that had died and felt less bad about it. "So you suspect it wasn't natural?"

Again Bardot's hazel eyes swept the area. "No. I do not think he passed peacefully in his sleep."

The excitement crept back into my voice as I fought the rising anticipation of a new murder in the village. Perhaps something I could help with? Even solve myself? "What makes you think foul play? Your detective instincts?"

"The vodka bottle smashed against a wall was a clue that things weren't as they seemed."

"Oh, was it a violent death, then? How did someone get in? How did he die?"

"We don't know yet. The body will be taken to Norwich for autopsy. There are no physical wounds, so the vodka bottle may mean nothing, but it seems suspicious. Guests heard raised voices last night, so it seems someone was with Georgie. But his body was tucked up in bed, so either the argument had nothing to do with it, or his body has been staged."

"Yuck, who would manhandle a corpse?"

Bardot sighed and drank long and deep from his coffee. "You'd be surprised."

I remembered that he had transferred from London. I knew he had been a homicide officer down there, and I wondered what he had seen. A shiver of fear ran through me that such evil was coming to our sleepy village. Twice in as many months.

"Do you have any leads yet on who might want to kill him?"

This time, Bardot did snort with laughter and waved a large, lightly tanned hand at the doors to the hotel. "Yes, and they were all conveniently camped right outside."

"Oh, come off it. They were angry, yes, but if they'd have wanted to kill Georgie they would have done it sooner and saved themselves weeks of miserable camping."

"They could have been waiting for an opportunity. Once the media circus died down and people lost interest, they made their move?"

I shook my head, thinking of the fruit thrower who had been terrified when he feared he was being accused of murder and the little old lady who was all talk. "I just don't see it. They were too passionately angry; they couldn't have waited. They would have found a way beforehand if they were planning to do it. If it was murder, I think it was someone with the patience of a bloody saint. Someone cold, calm, and calculated in the background. Bided their time, struck like a cobra."

Bardot's eyebrows, already slightly raised, vanished into his hairline. "Very profound. Did you get that from Crime Busters?"

"Oi! I'm just good at this stuff. My advice is free, take it or leave it."

"Thank you, Willow. I'll keep that in mind." He drank the last of his coffee and glanced down at it sadly.

I took it from him and shook the last drops around the base. "Want a refill?"

"That would be great, thanks."

"Wouldn't mind one myself," Sergeant Campbell said, becoming the second person to sneak up on me in the giant atrium.

"Not a problem," I assured him.

"Oh, are those for us?" Campbell asked, taking the bag clearly labelled "Bardot" from his junior officer. "Wonderful! I love cinnamon whirls."

I smiled sheepishly at Bardot as Campbell wandered off with a mouth full of pastry. "I'll bring you more of those, too."

"Thank you."

"We still need a coffee date, you know," I said softly.

"I know. And I do want to. I swear. It's just–"

"People keep getting murdered?" I said with a shy smile.

He returned it, and his face brightened momentarily. The shadows of death and exhaustion faded for just a moment. "Yeah, something like that."

"You live in North Walsham, right? Where are you staying? I imagine you'll be pulling all-nighters like the last murder."

"I…I've been…you know…" this time it was his turn to blush, his gorgeous smooth lightly tanned skin reddening under my gaze.

"Please tell me you're not sleeping on the floor of the police station?"

"Um…"

My eyes rolled back so far that I worried they wouldn't return. "I have a spare room. You'll be surrounded by my aunt's stuff I haven't got rid of yet, but the bed is easily uncovered. And far more comfortable than using your jacket as a pillow."

"Willow, I couldn't–"

"No excuses. I expect to see you tonight. I'll assume you'll be too late for dinner, but I'll throw in breakfast if that sweetens the deal. You know, if indeed I have to sweeten the offer of free accommodation."

"Are you sure? I might be pretty late."

I grabbed my keyring, unhooked a key and handed it to him. "This one is for the back door. I'll give you my spare front door one tomorrow morning. Then you don't have to worry about disturbing me."

He held the key tightly in his palm and raised it slightly to his chest. Was it my imagination, or was he holding it to his heart on purpose? "Thank you. You don't have any guard dogs I should know about?"

"No, just two cats," I said before I realised it.

"Cats are fine. I usually get on pretty well with cats. We come to an agreement of leaving one another alone."

"Then you'll fit in just fine," I said, panicking now that he would come to my home and expect to see a litter tray. Ghost cats don't produce waste like live cats.

He leaned a little closer as if coming in to kiss me, then seemed to remember himself and stepped back, coughing to cover his embarrassment. "Anyway, thank you again. That's very kind. I better go."

I nodded. "I'll bring you another coffee and new pastries. And then maybe I could get a peek inside the crime scene?"

He gave me a look.

"Alright, alright, I'll knock and close my eyes as you crack the door open. Deal?"

His smile returned. I wished I could make it stay there permanently.

"Deal."

Seven

Ooh, the M word again. Now, not that I like murders – I wasn't fond of my own – but this is just what Willow and the detective need. They worked so well together last time, I was so proud of my human for how she helped solve the case.

And secretly I think the detective liked having her help. He certainly thawed considerably.

This is just the thing to get them spending more time together! Wonderful.

--Thoughts from Luna

"Me! A murderer! My life is over."

Pippa and I spun around in fright. Isaac had just thrown open the door and lamented his life to the three people waiting for their orders.

"Uh, are you–" I began.

"No, I'm most definitely *not* alright!" He exclaimed, anticipating my next words. "I'm anything but alright. As if things weren't impossible enough before. I thought I'd been thrown a lifeline, but now...now things are even worse. How do I face my parents? How do I face the world? This is it. My life is over already."

He sank into a chair, and his lanky frame collapsed in on itself as he buried his head in his arms on the table.

The customers exchanged uncomfortable glances. Pippa nodded to him in a "go fix it before he scares off our paying customers" kind of way.

"Hey Isaac," I said, approaching him cautiously as one might a lion with tooth pain. "I assume this is about Georgie?"

"Of course!" Isaac said, his words muffled because his face was pressed against his arms.

I slipped into the chair opposite him and rested a comforting hand on his arm. "Do you want to talk about it?"

"No," he muttered miserably, then untangled himself and sat up straighter. "Well, maybe it will help. You see, it all happened so fast."

I nodded understandingly and discreetly motioned for Pippa to bring over a cup of coffee for him. It was hard to use covert military signals to say easy on the caffeine content since a) neither of us knew military hand signals, and b) military hand signals probably didn't have a specific sign for decaff.

"I was woken up by police banging on my door, then I was hauled out in my boxers and a t-shirt for questioning. Well, they let me get a robe, but it was still quite airy if you get what I mean. And they didn't even offer me a drink or anything. I have terribly bad breath in the morning, and I just wanted to brush my teeth, but they were having none of it!"

"Yes, they probably thought you would do a runner if they left you alone," I said.

"Where would I run to? And how would I run off on the second floor? Jump out of the window?"

"Fair point. Anyway, what happened next? What did they say?"

He sniffed miserably, using the corner of his sleeve to rub at his nose. "They said I was the last person to see Georgie alive and that they needed to know exactly what had happened last night when I gave him his medication and put him to bed."

"So he made it to bed as usual, then." I mused, not realising I'd done so aloud.

Isaac blinked in confusion, his glasses magnifying his eyes so that he resembled an owl. "Why wouldn't he have gone to bed?"

"Isaac, this is important. Was there a smashed bottle on the floor anywhere?"

"Smashed bottle?" he parroted, clearly not anticipating the question. Pausing to think, he pushed his glasses up his nose, then shook his head. "I don't remember seeing anything like that. I'd have commented and cleaned it up if I had seen it. Bottle of what? Medication?"

"Vodka."

"No, no, definitely not. Georgie couldn't drink on his medication."

A strange wave of calm washed over me, and I sat back in my chair to organise the scattered puzzle pieces that had been tossed in front of me. Slowly I began to slot them together to build the timeline of Georgie's final night.

Isaac had given Georgie his medication and got him ready for bed as usual, before leaving Georgie's room and retiring to his own for the evening.

Georgie had then gotten out of bed and had a visitor whom he argued with and who threw a vodka bottle at the wall.

Assumedly this mysterious visitor then murdered Georgie and fled.

"It's hopeless," Isaac wailed, elbows on the table and hands in his air, dislodging his large glasses. "The police think I did it. They're gathering evidence. I'm surprised they haven't arrested me already. We don't have the death penalty anymore, do we?" He asked desperately.

"No, we don't," I assured him. "And they'd need more evidence than you being the last person to see him alive if indeed that's even true."

Pippa approached and set down a mug in front of Isaac, who pounced like a cat catching prey.

"Careful, it's hot," Pippa tried to warn him, but he drank anyway.

"This might be my last cup of coffee as a free man," Isaac said, having drunk half of it in one scalding gulp. "Do they have hot drinks in prison?"

"Oh, for god's sake, man. Of course they do. And who says you're going to prison?" Pippa snapped, then turned on her heel and returned to the counter.

"She doesn't understand," Isaac muttered sadly into his cup. "Nobody understands. This is it. The end. Georgie was my only hope."

"What do you mean?" I pressed.

"He...he was...he didn't care that I..." Isaac shook his head as if the weight of it all was too much for him to shoulder. "He wasn't a good man. But he was good to me."

I filed that particular puzzle piece away for the future. It didn't fit into the bigger picture yet, but I was sure it was important. Isaac clearly wasn't ready to bare more of his soul, though; he was back to snuffling into his sleeve.

The rest of the working day passed smoothly. I did a few more coffee runs for the media troops, but then Oli took over when he arrived just before lunch, which gave my feet a welcome break.

By early afternoon I clocked off, leaving Oli with the late shift, and made my way home to do a little bit of tidying to ensure I hadn't left any underwear to dry on radiators or anything. If Bardot came stumbling in tired tonight, the last thing I wanted him to see was my comfy knickers greeting him – they weren't exactly elegant.

That was the plan, anyway. Things never turn out how we want, though, do they?

Catton Strawless isn't a massive village, but there are times when you can find yourself alone on the streets. Or not quite as alone as you'd like to be.

Perhaps it was my fault for not paying attention. I had my phone out and was mindlessly scrolling the news to see what was being reported on Georgie Weaver and if there were any new developments that might be useful to add to my building picture.

Maybe that inattention meant I didn't see the man stumbling out of the shrubbery ahead of me, then leaping to block my path.

When I finally noticed him, I screamed. Panic exploded like a firework in my chest, my breath caught in my throat, and my limbs went to jelly. My legs barely kept me standing, and the phone slipped from my hands, landing with a crack that promised a shattered screen. A groan escaped my lips: I had literally just bought it after Sally Ennis fed my old one into her waste disposal unit.

Fuelled by anger at the damage to my new phone, I was able to stand my ground instead of running away like my legs wanted to. "Who the hell are you? I know a policeman!" I added, in case that would deter him from whatever he had planned.

He took a few shaky steps forward, matching my retreat. He was tall, huge even, with muscles bulging in his arms and neck. Blood crusted under his nose, trailing down in rivulets to pool at the neck of his black t-shirt. His knuckles were scraped raw, and his hulking frame was hunched over. Dark shadows hung under his puffy eyes, and his skin was sallow and pale.

As he got closer, I smelled the terrible stench of alcohol which he wore like perfume. An underlying scent of body odour and general filth capped it off to make me recoil in disgust, bile rising in my throat.

Strangely, under the blood and filth, I recognised him as the man who had stormed into the hotel lobby the day before Georgie died.

Jawbreaker.

Sorry, *The* Jawbreaker.

"Wh am I?" he slurred.

The first syllable was so badly mangled that I wasn't one hundred per cent sure if he had asked where he was, who he was or what he was.

"You're Ricky Moreno, aren't you?" I asked.

Clarity began to emerge in his clouded, bloodshot eyes, and he slowly nodded his large bald head. "Yeah. Yeah, I am. Where the hell am I? Why did I wake up in a field? What happened?"

"I really couldn't say," I said, taking another tentative step away from him. "But I think you need to find somewhere to sleep and sober up. Somewhere with a shower."

"Room. Shower." He mumbled, then drew in a sharp breath. "Hotel! That tosser! I'll kill him! I'll kill him, I will! I did kill him? Did I already? I can't remember."

He stumbled toward me a few steps, and I had to leap back to avoid his grabbing hands reaching out for me.

"I have no idea what you're talking about," I lied. I could only assume that he was talking about Georgie. A few more puzzle pieces slipped into place: Ricky had promised to revisit Georgie that night. It looked like I had found the owner of the smashed vodka bottle.

"He wouldn't pay up. He owed me! The stingy old bugger owed me. All that I did for him in prison. He would have been killed in there. Would have been killed!" Ricky roared, anger blazing in his eyes as he stood up straight.

He was a good foot or so taller than me I realised with a fresh stab of panic that constricted my chest and made it hard to draw a calming breath. Deep blue oceans. Waves on a beach. The gentle lull of dolphins out to sea. I tried to recall a meditation I'd heard on an app, but the waves came crashing up like a squall when Ricky leapt for me again.

"Argh!"

This time I wasn't quick enough to get out of his way. Well, that's what I liked to think. Really my foot caught on uneven pavement, and I fell back, cracking my head on the path and stunning my elbow painfully.

"Get off her!" someone screamed.

Oh, thank god, someone had spotted us.

"Damn, the filth!" Ricky yelped, and the large shadow that had loomed over me vanished.

"Willow! Willow, are you ok?" Bardot skidded to a stop and dropped to his knees, his hands strong and gentle as he helped me sit up.

"I'm fine, I promise. You need to go and get Ricky, though. He needs to be questioned. Arrested maybe. I don't know." I winced as my skull throbbed with pain, and nausea rose in my throat.

"Who?" Bardot asked, glancing down the street. "That man?"

"Yes! Yes, he's...oww, painful. He somehow saw Georgie the night he died. He was in the room. I think it's his vodka bottle."

Bardot wasn't moving. His hands were feather soft as he parted my hair. I felt something warm and sticky on my scalp.

"I need to get you to a hospital," Bardot muttered.

"What about Ricky?" I moaned. The spots in front of my eyes were becoming more pronounced, dancing in swirling patterns that were very distracting.

"Sod that. He's gone now, anyway, I'll put out a search request in a minute. Can you stand?"

"Yes," I said confidently before promptly passing out in his arms.

The last thing I heard was Bardot calling my name, begging me to open my eyes. But I simply couldn't.

Eight

Oh goodness! I hadn't expected my human to be injured. This is a terrible turn of events. That horrible man who hurt her, Loki and I went searching for him but could find no trace.

Still, sometimes these things happen for a reason. Willow is still alive and the handsome detective went with her to hospital. Perhaps this will help him realise his feelings. I will leave her in his very capable hands while Loki and I continue our search.

--Thoughts from Luna

Slowly I began to wake.

Dragging my mind into the waking world was like swimming through quicksand; the harder I tried, the more difficult the task became. So I stopped trying and let my consciousness float and drift in its own time.

Other senses returned. The warmth of the sheets beneath me. The distant scent of cooked cabbage. A faint metallic tang in my mouth.

As I woke up, my body began responding. Like a computer switching on each of its parts and doing a roll call to let me know everything was present and working. Feet? Check. Arms? Left one was painful. Head? Owwww!

"Ugh," I groaned, forcing my eyes open. They were gritty and warm, and every blink was like exfoliating my eyeballs.

"She lives," said a soft voice, blissfully pitched low so as not to disturb my throbbing headache.

"She does?" I asked, not entirely convinced. Although if this was heaven, then I wanted my money back.

"Lay still. You have a mild concussion."

"Nothing mild about it," I muttered, wincing as a lightning bolt of pain darkened my vision and made me want to throw up.

Inch by inch, I turned my head on the thin, lumpy pillow to see Bardot. He was sitting on a simple plastic chair, still in uniform, with his short dark hair mussed from running his hands through it. The lights were out in the room, but artificial white light spilt in from the corridor.

"Hospital?" I asked him.

He nodded, leaning toward me, resting his elbows on his knees, and clasping his hands together. "In Norwich, yes. I followed the ambulance here."

"Oh yeah, Ricky," I said, closing my eyes to dredge up a memory. It was blurry. "Did you catch him?"

"No, but we have officers searching for him. From what you said, he's now a person of interest in the Weaver case, so we need his statement. Not to mention I have a set of cuffs with his name on them for what he did to you."

"Yeah," I said softly, wondering what drugs I had been given to make me this muzzy or if the head injury was to blame. Everything felt dull. When I looked at Bardot, it was as if the silvery light was coming from him.

"You glow," I said.

"Sorry?" he said, leaning closer.

"Glow. Like an angel." The words tumbled from my lips. "A pretty angel."

"Ah," he coughed discreetly. "I think they gave you some morphine."

"Excellent." I smiled and reached out an arm for him. "Kiss me goodnight?"

"I think it's probably best if I leave. I just wanted to make sure you were ok."

"I'm ok."

"Good. Good." He seemed not to know what to do with himself, so my free hand grabbed for the hem of his jacket. Gently he detangled my fingers. "Is it still alright if I spend the night in your guest room?"

"Yeah, of course."

"Thank you, Willow. I'll feed the cats, make sure they're ok."

"They're dead. Doesn't matter."

"Dead?" Was the last word I heard as I drifted off again into a deep sleep.

The next time I woke up, the pain was a dull, constant throb in the back of my skull. The fogginess (and pain-relieving benefits) of the morphine had left my system.

A nurse helped me sit up, eat breakfast, take my vital signs and then get dressed. It was nice to be out of the rough hospital gown, even if the clothes were the ones I had been admitted in, so they were dirty from my fall.

Next, a doctor arrived and told me that the scans were clear and there was no fracture or bleeding, so I could go home if I had someone to drive me and stay with me.

I called Pippa using a phone borrowed from a kind nurse, as my own was smashed and unresponsive.

"Don't panic," I started the call off with.

"I *wasn't* panicked. But by saying don't panic, you've made me think that actually I should be panicking," Pippa said. "Should I panic?"

"No! But I need you to come and pick me up, please. I'm in the hospital."

"Oh god. Now I am panicking."

Pain pulsated at the base of my skull. "Pippa, please don't panic. I fell and hit my head yesterday when this huge drunk guy lunged for me."

"I'm sending Oli right now! I don't think I can drive in this state..."

An hour later, I was hobbling across the Norwich Hospital car park toward Oli's ancient silver Volkswagen. Oli's hands were shoved in his pockets, and his head was tipped up to watch a flock of seagulls fly over, and probably poo on, the parked cars.

"Thanks, Oli."

"No problem. Pippa is beside herself; I wouldn't want her driving in that state. She'd end up in the bed next to you."

"I told her not to panic," I muttered, feeling terrible for causing so much trouble for my friends.

"And you know that'll just make her panic more," Oli said with a smile, then held the door open so I could gingerly climb inside. "She's calm as a monk until someone is hurt."

The headrest was unusable, as it touched the exact spot on my head that had been stitched up and felt bruised to hell and back. So for the whole fifty-minute trip, I sat bolt-upright, wincing at every little bump in the road. The tyres seemed to search out the potholes, and each one felt as deep as the Grand Canyon to my poor battered brain.

Oli took me to the front door of the café then drove off to go and find somewhere to park.

"Oh, thank god!" Pippa yelled, rushing around from the counter to hug me gently. "Are you ok? What happened? Did they get the guy that did this to you?"

"Well, technically, I tripped, so he didn't hurt me. Just surprised me. I wasn't sure what he was going to do. I think he's a suspect."

Pippa led me into the staff room and onto a soft fabric cream sofa. I explained what had happened, what I had found out, and that Bardot had tasked his officers to look out for Ricky so he could be questioned.

"So, in a way, I helped with the investigation," I finished proudly.

"You'll be the death of me, Willow," Pippa sighed, shaking her head. Her hands clutched mine tightly; as if she let go, I'd fade away. "Please tell me you're not doing this on purpose?"

"What cracking my head open like a coconut? No, that was definitely not on purpose."

"Investigating," Pippa whispered as if the word itself might summon a devil. "Like last time with Eleanor. You're not investigating this on your own, are you? Last time you almost got yourself killed. This time you end up in the hospital. Ever heard the phrase, "if at first you don't succeed, police work is not for you"? You're not even getting paid for it, so what's the point in risking your neck?"

"I can help. I've *already* helped."

"Willow, we have police for a reason. They investigate and keep us safe. So don't go putting yourself in danger, right?"

"Right," I mumbled.

Pippa grabbed the rainbow patchwork blanket from the back of the sofa and tucked it around me. "I'll pop in every few minutes to check on you. I expect to see you on this sofa each time."

"Even if I need the loo?"

Pippa tutted and walked off, shaking her head. The door clicked shut, and I was left in silence, only the humming of something electrical as white background noise to lull me to sleep.

Nine

I'm aloof – I'm a cat, it's my job – but that doesn't mean I'm not perceptive. I often follow my dozy human around and when I saw her attacked by that brute I leaped into action.

Sort of.

It happened so fast and I had to check she was alive before pursuing. For such a big man, he escaped very quickly. The stench of stale alcohol helped me follow him for a while, Luna trailing in my wake.

Eventually we found him hiding out in an old tin shed on a set of allotments. Just sitting, hugging his knees among the old flowerpots and cobwebs.

Humans are very odd, but he seems to be staying put for now.

--Thoughts from Loki

It took a long moment to figure out where I was when I woke up. I'd never woken up on the sofa in the back office before, and the ceiling was unfamiliar. The blanket was soft and warm, crocheted by Pippa's grandmother and gave that kind of old familiarity that magically wraps you up and makes you feel better.

But I was on a mission: my head was pounding. I needed medication.

Blindly I dug around in the little paper bag that had been issued to me and took out the co-codamol. Bah, they hadn't sent me home with any morphine. I downed two pills with the glass of water Pippa had kindly left out for me, then lay on my side to avoid aggravating the injury and waited for them to kick in.

And waited.

And waited.

Finally, fed up with feeling sick with pain, I rolled off the sofa and stumbled into the café. "Pippa?"

"Darling, you look awful," was her answer.

"Thanks. The painkillers aren't working. Have you got anything else I can take?"

"Only paracetamol, and I think they put that in your co-codamol," Pippa said. "You need some ibuprofen, and I haven't got any I'm afraid."

"It's fine. I'll pop to the pharmacy. It's only down the road."

"You will not," Pippa yelped. "Not alone. Let me pack up, and I'll go."

"I want the fresh air," I complained. But I had to admit I still felt a little unsteady on my feet. "How about we go together?"

Pippa seemed less unhappy with that option, so we flipped the sign, locked the door and shuffled at my pace down to the pharmacy at the end of the road.

The pharmacy smelled sterile in its cleanliness, with a hint of mint. The lights were so bright it felt like I was under a police interrogation lamp. I didn't often come into the pharmacy but vaguely recognised the young woman behind the counter. My fogged brain grasped for a name, but when I got closer to the counter, I could read her name tag.

"Hi, Chloe," I said, pretending I had remembered it of my own accord. It was the girl that Isaac liked, though I had no idea why since her face was permanently set into a scowl.

"How can I help?" she asked, straight to business.

Chloe was younger than me, seemingly too young to be doing the job of a trained pharmacist, but her brushed silver name tag and framed diploma on the wall identified her as fully qualified. Her sharp, cat-like green eyes were already assessing me, working out what I needed. Her face was an inexpressive mask of the indifference of youth.

"Painkillers?" she guessed.

"Please," I rasped. "Ibuprofen. Max strength. I'm already on co-codamol."

Chloe nodded, her deep blue pixie-cut hair rippling with the action. As if a half-conscious patient in her pharmacy was an everyday occurrence. She turned, reached out a hand and picked up a box without pausing as if she could do this in her sleep.

"Best to take them with food, no more than three doses every twenty-four hours," she said while ringing up the item. "Five ninety-nine. Cash or card?"

"Card," I said, digging into my pocket. "Oh...no..."

My phone was still smashed. My cards were linked to it, so my primary payment method was gone. Whining softly, I jabbed my phone's power button, shaking the device in my attempts to coax it back to life. But it was well and truly dead. My shiny new phone's life had been tragically cut short.

Despair filled my lungs so that I could barely breathe. My body turned to lead, and my knees almost buckled. I just wanted the painkillers. That was all I wanted. Why was this happening? Why me?

Pippa reached over and waved her phone at the card reader, and the transaction was done.

"Thank you," I muttered pitifully.

Pippa patted my shoulder delicately. Before I knew it, a little paper cup of water was being pushed across the counter next to the box of pills. Chloe even went so far as to whip open the box and expertly pierce the film with her thumbnail, freeing two for me.

"Thank you. Thank you." I gulped them down and chased them with water.

"Good friend you have there. Wish I had a friend that could magic away my pharmacy student debts." Chloe leaned against the counter. "Been pretty dead in here today anyway."

"Exact opposite for us," Pippa said. "Café business booms when there's a murder in town."

"Murder?" Chloe's eyes flew wide, and her already pale skin turned ashen. For a moment, I worried that she would be the one to faint or throw up.

Pippa's hands flew to her mouth. "Oops. Well, I think the rumours are flying anyway. Don't worry, darling, it's probably a revenge thing, not a mass murder serial killer kind of thing. It was Georgie Weaver. You know, that guy who was released early from prison and came to stay at the Windmill Inn. Did you hear about him?"

A shadow passed over Chloe's face as she lowered her head. "Course I knew about him. Everyone around here does. He's famous for all the wrong reasons, right? He destroyed lives and got people killed. He was a monster and got what was coming to him."

Pippa's hands slowly slid from her mouth to hang at her sides. "Well, yes, he was definitely an evil man. But did he deserve to be killed?"

"Some people deserve it. That monster should have rotted in prison. They gave him a pathetic nine years, and he's done about half. He was on the run living it large with other people's money for years. He should have been made to spend every single hour of that nine-year sentence in prison, even if he was sick. They should have let him decompose in his cell."

The following silence was broken only by the ticking clock above the cosmetic display and a dog barking outside.

"That's certainly one way of looking at it," I said.

Another long silence stretched. The dog got bored of barking, and we were left with just the ticking clock.

"Anyway, remember to eat something to go with that ibuprofen," Chloe said, her cheeks regaining their usual pale peach colour and her voice lowering back to bored-teenage level.

Something a woman in her twenties should not be able to pull off but Chloe did it well.

"Thanks. Yes." I said.

"Yes. Thanks." Pippa said.

We edged away toward the door, smiles fixed on our faces, then as soon as we were out the door, we hurried back to the café.

"Where have you *been?*" Isaac wailed as we approached.

"We've literally been gone for ten minutes," Pippa said, unlocking the door and entering with a ring of the bell above us.

I hadn't realised how loud the bell was before my head injury.

Even dizzy with the pain, I couldn't resist pressing him for info. "Why? What's happened? Are they going to make an arrest?"

"No, I just need coffee," Isaac said, blinking owlishly at me and readjusting his glasses.

"I realise this is a terrible way to do business, but if you were that desperate for caffeine, other cafés are available, you know?" Pippa said.

"I know..." Isaac said, trailing off and staring down at his scruffy trainers. His glasses slipped down his nose again. Why didn't he get them adjusted to fit correctly?

Pippa shot him a strange look but began making his usual double espresso.

"Actually I..." Isaac began, his voice catching. "I don't...I can't...I was wondering..."

"Spit it out, man," Pippa said.

"Do you do a loyalty scheme? Like, buy five get one free or something?"

"No. We don't. Maybe in the future." Pippa's eyes narrowed at him. "Why?"

"I just, um, I've been a loyal customer," his hands fiddled with his glasses, pushing them up the bridge of his nose only for them to fall down again when he avoided Pippa's intense gaze and went back to staring at his feet. "Thought maybe this one might be free? Maybe? Please?"

"Free?" Pippa asked as if she had never heard the word before.

"I don't...have money at the moment," he said, with the ease of someone passing a gallstone.

"You can't get into your room?" Pippa asked, understanding blossoming on your face. "Because of the police investigation."

For a moment, Isaac looked torn, and then he nodded enthusiastically. "Exactly. But I really need a coffee, and since I've been here so often, I thought maybe–"

Pippa sighed dramatically but gave him a warm smile. "Oh, go on then. This once. Just don't go telling everyone."

The way the tension melted from his shoulders was almost sad, and he gratefully took the coffee and sat himself down to drink it carefully, savouring every drop.

Having watched the whole exchange from a seat at the same table Isaac had chosen, I decided that my headache was fading enough to ask a few more questions without taxing myself too much. Or maybe my nosiness bolstered my pain threshold.

"So, are they still there? The police?"

"Yeah. They moved out the body late last night, but the crime scene guys are still padding around everywhere in their white suits. And I was told I couldn't leave, but they won't reimburse my hotel room fees."

"What's their working theory?" I asked.

"How should I know?" he asked, staring down at the dregs of his coffee and clearly wishing he hadn't drunk it so fast. "Not like they talk to me. I suppose I'm the prime suspect since I was the last person to see him alive. Surprised I haven't been locked up yet. At least I wouldn't have to pay for my room if I was in a cell."

"That's a depressing way of looking at it," I said, a frown crumpling my face as I watched him. "Isaac, did you kill Georgie?"

"No!"

"Then you haven't got anything to worry about. They'll figure it out. Apparently, the room next door heard arguing. I don't know when, but it might have been after you left Georgie. So you might not be the last person to have seen him alive."

"Maybe."

"What about you? Did you hear any arguments?" I asked.

"No. I didn't hear a thing. But then I went straight to bed so I could have slept through it, I guess?" He heaved a sigh and slumped in his seat. "What's the use? My life is over anyway."

"Because nobody will hire a nurse who's suspected of murder?" I asked.

He paused for a second, then nodded. "Yeah."

"Well, I guess the police are waiting for the autopsy results. They might be your saving grace. Maybe all this fuss is for nothing, and he really did just die naturally?"

"Maybe," Isaac muttered, gazing longingly into his empty cup again.

I rolled my eyes and leaned over the back of the chair. "Pippa, bring him another one, for god's sake. I'll pay. When I fix my phone."

"Thanks. That's really kind."

"You look like you could use it," I said, turning back to him. "And I wanted to ask one more question. Did you know anything about someone called Ricky Moreno? Or maybe you knew him as The Jawbreaker?"

Isaac shook his head. "Never heard of him."

My shoulders slumped, and I realised I'd paid for a coffee for nothing. I had felt so sure Isaac would know something. "He was in prison with Georgie. Georgie never mentioned him? At all?"

"Georgie didn't talk to me much except to order me around," Isaac said, tucking and untucking his long legs. "He snapped a lot. Told me the tv was always too low and accused me of turning the volume down. Told me the drugs were no good, that I wasn't giving him enough of the "good stuff", as he called it."

"Morphine?" I said dreamily, wishing I had some of that right now instead of co-codamol and ibuprofen.

Isaac nodded. "Nothing I did was right."

"Why put up with that?"

"Jobs a job," Isaac shrugged. "Someone had to put up with him."

"What prison was Georgie in again? The one in Norwich, right?" I said.

"Yeah, he was in the B wing. B-2. I saw it on his discharge papers."

"B-2," I repeated, mulling over the start of a plan in my mind. A plan I was going to need help with. Because with my head injury driving myself into Norwich was a terrible idea.

I glanced over at Pippa, who was fixing me with a look.

"Road trip?" I asked.

She huffed a sigh but didn't disagree.

Road trip. Excellent.

Ten

I sent Loki off to keep watch of the brute of a man hiding away in the shed. Loki is smart, I'll give him that but clueless in matters of the heart.

The wonderful scents of the sizzling risotto were clear the moment I walked into the house and what it meant was obvious to me. So I made Loki leave so that he couldn't ruin this perfect night.

I stayed to watch, of course. Just to make sure it went alright.

--Thoughts from Luna

Pippa, who had turned into my mother, refused to drive me the same day. Something about too much excitement already or something and the fact I'd only been discharged from the hospital that morning. Whatever the case, she made me promise to get a good night's sleep, and she would leave Oli in charge of the café and take me to prison in the morning.

I had no option but to agree.

She walked me home, hovering the whole way, insisting that she would stay the night with me. She saw the bright golden light in the kitchen window as we approached.

"Did you leave the light on?" she asked.

"No," I said, confused. "Do burglars turn lights on?"

"They must need to see what they're stealing somehow," Pippa reasoned.

Cautiously we tried the front door; it opened easily, swinging invitingly on its hinges. Pippa and I exchanged a worried glance. She took out her phone, ready to call the police. We crept in, closing the door behind us.

A pale streak flashed in front of me.

"Argh!" I yelped, almost crashing into Pippa as I leapt back.

"What's wrong?" she demanded.

I could hardly tell her that the ghost of a dead cat had run in front of me and disappeared through a wall, could I?

"Sorry, I thought I saw something."

A thud from the kitchen made us both jump again, and we grabbed hold of one another as we held our breath and listened for more sounds. There was scraping, then chopping. Chopping? What a strange sound for a burglar to make. Unless they were cutting up my belongings to make them easier to carry?

"Stay behind me," Pippa whispered, bravely forging forward and brandishing her mobile phone like a weapon.

Inching toward the kitchen door, she nudged it with her toe so that it swung inward, then took a deep breath and jumped into the room.

"Don't move!" she cried.

Quickly I hurried to join her, ready to be her backup or at least grab the phone and call for help if the burglar attacked her first.

I was met with a startled Detective Constable Bardot, who raised his hands with a bemused expression ghosting his face.

"You got me?" he asked.

Memories flooded back as if a dam had burst. "Oh, right! I offered him my spare room while he's working the murder case."

"Who says it's a murder?" Bardot muttered, but there was no fight in his words. He knew by now that rumours spread like wildfire in a small community like Catton Strawless.

Pippa glared at me for forgetting I had a guest, then slowly straightened up and slipped her phone into her back pocket. "Well, let that be a lesson to you."

"I consider myself duly taught. May I move yet? I wouldn't want the risotto to burn."

"Risotto?" I asked hopefully.

"I thought it was only fair I cooked tonight, with you still recovering. I will have to go back out later, but I thought I could take a couple of hours to shower, make dinner and check that you were ok."

"That's really kind of you. Thanks." A warmth blossomed in my chest that he was doing something so kind. And that he genuinely wanted to and was worried about me.

"Well, looks like I'm a third wheel," Pippa said, with a discreet wink to me that had the tips of my ears heating up. "I'll leave you to dinner. Willow, call me if you need anything."

"Yeah. And thanks for today," I said distractedly, realising after she had gone that her number was safely stored on my destroyed mobile phone.

The hiss of sizzling rice serenaded me as I sat at the little dining table in my kitchen and watched Bardot as he worked. With practised ease, he scraped veg into the pan at the exact right times so that everything would be cooked together. The creamy scent of chicken and mushrooms wafted over and piqued my appetite.

"Shame we haven't got any wine. Not that I think I should drink," I added as an afterthought.

"Check the bag," Bardot nodded to a supermarket carrier bag hooked over the back of the other dining chair. Inside was a glass bottle of posh-looking sparkling water.

I collected two wine glasses and filled them to the brim. I sipped at mine, the bubble tickling my tongue, as Bardot heaped risotto onto two plates and added a slice of toasted rustic bread that had been warming in the oven.

"Wow. This looks amazing," I said as he placed mine in front of me and handed over a fork.

"My grandmother taught me to cook. When she died, I inherited her favourite cookbook. She crossed out huge sections on every single page and revised every recipe," he said with a chuckle. "Always did know best, my nana."

"Sounds like she was a fantastic woman."

Bardot nodded, his mouth full of rice, so he was unable to answer properly.

We ate peacefully for a few moments, and I enjoyed the food. The chicken was tender, the mushrooms were not slimy, and the sauce had the right consistency. "If this is a Nana Bardot recipe, then whatever she changed from the original was for the better."

"It is indeed, and I'm sure she'd be pleased to hear it," Bardot said, mopping up the sauce with his bread. "Did you go to work today?"

My fork paused midway to my mouth. "Uh, well, I was at work. But I wasn't working. Pippa insisted I nap on the sofa so she could keep an eye on me."

Bardot nodded. "That's fine. So long as you weren't pushing yourself or doing anything reckless."

"Who me?" I said innocently, popping a mouthful of chicken and rice in my mouth to avoid having to say anything more.

"I mean it. You had a run-in with a known criminal yesterday."

"He didn't hurt me; I tripped. Have you found him yet?"

"No," Bardot said with a frown. "He's officially a wanted man, though. I certainly have some questions for him."

"About the murder that's not officially a murder?"

Bardot groaned and swirled his fork in the remnants of his dinner. "It'll be officially a murder tomorrow. Lab reports just came back. That's why I need to work after dinner, prepare for a media briefing tomorrow and question someone we just brought in."

"How did he die?" I asked, dinner forgotten as I leaned closer.

Bardot drew a long breath, warring with himself over whether to tell me. Ever the proper policeman, he knew that it would be plastered over the news soon enough. "Medication overdose."

"Drugs?" I asked, startled. "He died of a drug overdose? How did he get them? How did Isaac not know?"

"Prescription medication, not drugs," Bardot corrected. "There was an elevated amount of morphine in his bloodstream. The autopsy shows he died of pulmonary oedema – fluid in the lungs for the layperson. He had advanced lung cancer which wouldn't have helped his chances."

"Oh. Morphine." I sat back in my chair, strangely dissatisfied with the cause of death. "So the big man, The Jawbreaker, that rules him out, right? Surely he'd have just punched him to death?"

"Not necessarily," Bardot said, raising his glass and taking a measured sip as if it were alcoholic. "The morphine had been left in Georgie's room that night. If Isaac left before The Jawbreaker got into Georgie's room, then The Jawbreaker could have decided to use that as a murder weapon."

My face screwed up, betraying my thoughts on that theory. "Oh, come on, the guy was drunk as a skunk, and fighting is in his blood. He wouldn't use such a delicate method."

"I can't discount anything," Bardot said. "But there wasn't a mark on Georgie's body to indicate physical violence, so either The Jawbreaker varied his modus operandi, or he's not the killer."

"Or," I mused, thinking aloud, "Georgie killed himself? If the morphine was left there, he could have been overcome with guilt for what he did and took his own life?"

Bardot raised a slender eyebrow.

I frowned. "Ok, I admit he didn't seem quick to repent. It could have been an accident, I suppose? He was in pain, saw the drugs there, and just injected without knowing how much he should have taken?"

"That's a more likely scenario if Georgie administered it," Bardot said. "But either The Jawbreaker or Georgie feel like I'm trying too hard to make them fit. There is a much more obvious, neater solution."

"Isaac." The nurse's name slipped out of my mouth. Then I sat bolt upright as if I'd been electrocuted. "Isaac? No way! No, no, he wouldn't. Why would he? He was so grateful for the job."

Bardot shrugged and shovelled up the last mouthful of rice. "I can't say I've established motive yet, but that's what I intend to do tonight."

Panic constricted my chest. I felt a tightening as if my lungs had inflated too much. "Isaac is the one you arrested?"

"Just taken in for questioning," Bardot defended, dabbing at his lips with a napkin he had produced from a pack in the supermarket bag. "I need to establish timelines to see if Isaac was the last person to see Georgie alive. I need to know why the morphine was left in the patient's room. And I need to see his records for the administration of medication."

"What about The Jawbreaker?"

"I can't question him if I can't find him," Bardot said, annoyingly practical. "When we find him, I will have plenty of questions for him too."

Panic began to set in, an irrational need to help Isaac. He had looked so lost, so upset. "But you said someone heard an argument that night. Surely that's got to be investigated?"

"The room next door heard two men arguing. Isaac is also a man. For all we know, The Jawbreaker never made it into Georgie's room at all, and it was Isaac with whom he had a fight."

I had nothing more to say. The wind was well and truly knocked out of my sails. I crumpled in my seat, my head throbbing and my body exhausted.

"Go get some sleep," Bardot said softly, his warm, strong hand on my shoulder. "Call me if you need me. I'll be back in a few hours."

I nodded miserably, once again forgetting that my phone was unusable and the holder of all my contact numbers.

"Thanks for dinner. You didn't have to do that."

"I know," he said, slipping his dark jacket over his deep navy uniform. "But it was my pleasure. I hope we can do it again sometime."

"Tomorrow?" I asked. "You can stay here as long as you need if it makes it easier than travelling home every night. Especially if you're doing late nights."

"That would be great. I'll see you later, Willow."

"Bye."

Eleven

Perfect! Absolutely wonderful.

And the detective is staying longer, even better. I quite like having another human about the house. When I was with Eleanor she had a huge mansion and for the most part we were alone. The halls were cold and silent, despite my human being full of life. Even when Parker was there it was too empty.

So two humans in this little house is perfect. Although a third tiny one would be even better! But I'm getting ahead of myself, it was just dinner.

--Thoughts from Luna

My dreams were vivid. Perhaps the cocktail of painkillers or the head injury itself contributed. Still, as I wandered through a jungle in my dreams, I swear I could feel the squidge of soft mud beneath my boots, taste the sweetness of flora in the air, and feel the cloying humidity bead on my skin.

A snake slithered down from a branch, its pink forked tongue waggling at me and its yellow eyes spinning to hypnotise me.

Not to be fooled, I turned away, pushing giant rubbery leaves aside as I wove off the beaten track and forged my own way.

Branches whipped my cheeks, and my breath came out in little puffs from the effort of shoving aside leaves that became larger, thicker, and heavier with every step. My feet slipped on the mud, which seemed to get slipperier the further I ventured from the path until I eventually reached out with my foot and felt nothing.

With a gasp, I plunged into the water, which was cool and refreshing after the hot, stuffy jungle. I swam deeper, able to see everything with perfect clarity. A shoal of seahorses swam past, and I didn't even pause to wonder what they were doing in a jungle lake.

After hours of swimming without breathing, I resurfaced, but the jungle had gone. Or rather, had been destroyed. I slowly emerged from the lake to find the ground ashen and the trees burned to blackened stumps. The air was heavy and thick with smoke.

A strange rhythmic thud and a leopard appeared from the fallen burned trees, his green eyes glowing hungrily. My feet had sunk into the fine, sandy ash, and I couldn't move. The leopard barrelled into me, pushing me to the ground and landing with a heavy thump on my chest, driving the air from my lungs.

I woke, struggling to breathe and realised the leopard was real.

"Loki, get off," I muttered.

Ok, maybe not a leopard, but he was still annoying when he wanted to be.

Now that I was awake, Loki resumed his ghostly state so that he weighed nothing, but he remained on my chest, glaring down at me with bright green eyes that glowed in the darkness of my bedroom. Just like the leopard in my dreams.

"I swear to god, if you've figured out how to infiltrate my dreams, I'm calling a cat exorcist," I mumbled.

Now that Loki was non-corporeal, I could turn over to my side and pull the blanket up to tuck around my chin.

"Mrow," Loki said, unhappy that I was going back to sleep.

"Loki, it's not even two in the morning. I'm sorry I wasn't here yesterday, but I had a pretty good excuse. And now I want to sleep, so you'll have to go without any treats tonight."

"Mrow," Loki said, turning solid long enough to latch his claws onto the edge of my blanket and pull at it.

"Stop that! You'll leave holes in it," I snapped, emerging from my cocoon of warmth to rescue my blanket from his claws.

He looked at me smugly as if he'd won a battle.

"I'm not getting up. I'm not," I said, laying back down and pulling the blanket over my head, this time to show I meant business.

Of course, Loki viewed that as an act of throwing down the gauntlet of challenge.

For a few blissful moments, all was silent. The throbbing in my skull began to fade as my body relaxed and sank against the pillow again. The room's coolness soothed me, my eyes closed, and darkness crept in to claim me.

"MeoooooooOOOOOoooow," Loki sang. With accompanying backing music.

My doors have little stoppers screwed to the walls to stop the door from banging and taking off a chunk of plaster. The stoppers are tightly wound wire coils with a little rubber tip. They are flexible. Loki loves them because, using his paw, he can pull the stopper to one side as far as it will go and then let it free. It will then spring from side to side with dizzying speed while making a loud off-key *twang* that echoes in a dark, silent bedroom.

"Loki, you little bugger, stop it!" I yelled, then groaned as pain exploded at the back of my head.

"MeoooooooOOOOOoooow."

"No more!"

"MeoooooooOOOOOoooow."

"Fine! Fine." I kicked the covers back, tangling my legs in the process. Angrily I freed myself, snapped on the bedroom light and jammed my feet into my slippers.

"Mrow," Loki said proudly. I swear he was grinning. I know cats can't grin, but he *was* grinning.

Carefully I emerged from my bedroom, memories flooding back and suddenly scared that Bardot would have heard me yelling at a dead cat. But the guest bedroom door was wide open, and the room was dark and empty.

I spared a thought for Isaac, perhaps still being interrogated. I didn't think him capable of murder. But then, how well did

I really know him? He'd been talking about prison. Maybe a guilty conscience was eating away at him.

"Mrow," Loki said. Translating roughly to: *hurry up, human.*

"You won; I'm up. But I'm not going to hurry," I hissed.

Downstairs we went. As I rustled through the cupboards for the cookie jar of PsyTreats I keep for them, I heard another set of paws on the kitchen tiles.

"Mow?" Luna asked. Translated as: *Dinner? Lunch? Breakfast?*

"Yeah yeah. You're both way too spoiled. You know that?" I asked grumpily as I dumped a few treats into their bowls. Happily, they crowded and began munching away, their tails winding to the sky happily as the little magical treats nourished and gave them warmth and love.

I shook the jar pitifully, barely more than crumbs left. I'd need to whip up a new batch soon, or there'd be riots from my feline housemates.

As I bent to replace the near-empty tub in the cupboard, I heard a flowerpot outside the window tip over, the tell-tale shattering of pottery smashing.

"Loki, what are you..." I stopped. As I turned around, expecting to see Loki gone, I found him still munching away at his treats.

A chill ran through me, and my stomach clenched as I tried to peer out the window. The angle was wrong; I couldn't see anything but the trees to the right of the house. The window was pretty high, with plenty of space for someone to be crouched directly under it and for me never to know unless I got close enough to look out.

Trying to move slowly and soundlessly, I crept out of the kitchen and started for the stairs, intending to call Bardot. Or the police. Or anyone. But no sooner had my foot reached the first step when the shattered screen of my poor phone sprang to mind. I didn't have a landline. There would be no calls for help.

"Okay, keep calm," I told myself, trying to push down the panic rising like the tide within me. The panic led to increased pain, fogging my mind and making it hard to think. A negative feedback loop that had me spiralling into a panic attack.

"Get a grip!" I snapped. "Might have been a fox. Or the wind."

That calmed me a little. I lived in rural North Norfolk, and foxes were not uncommon. It could have even been a neighbour's cat of the living variety. Maybe even a hedgehog. Could they push over heavy pots? They're probably stronger than they looked.

Just as the rational calm was wrapping me up like a comforting blanket, a new noise tugged that blanket from me. A distinct noise that was certainly no fox or cat. Or hedgehog.

The front door handle was rattling. Someone was trying to get in.

Bardot? But he had a key. Why would he keep trying the handle without using the key? And if he was struggling, he could knock. Unless he thought I was asleep and didn't want to disturb me.

Inching toward the door, the handle rattled again, then stopped. By the time I reached the door and peered through the spyhole, nobody was there. If it was Bardot, would he leave? Where would he go at this time of night? If he drove back to North Walsham at this hour, he might fall asleep at the wheel.

Against my better judgement, I grabbed the key from the hook at the door and unlocked it, pushing open the door and stepping out into the cold dark evening.

The porch step was cold on my feet, even in my slippers. The yellow porch light was horribly bright, almost blinding me in its intensity. The air was still, the night close; it felt like I was on the set of a stage play.

And then a shadow in the darkness. A movement in the near distance.

"Bardot?" I called.

Nothing. Fear gripped me like a vice. My instincts told me to get inside and lock the door.

Stupidly I tried again. "Thomas?"

Heavy footsteps stumbled toward me. A towering, hulking figure stepped into the pool of golden light. His t-shirt was filthy and torn. Blood still crusted at his nostrils. Even from a few paces away, I could smell the stench of booze and stale sweat.

My fight-or-flight instinct finally kicked in, and I leapt back into the safety of my house and slammed the door as fast as possible.

Not fast enough.

When I glanced down, I saw a black boot wedged in the gap, and no matter how hard I kicked it with my pathetic fluffy slippered foot, I couldn't dislodge it.

Meaty fingers appeared on the edge of the door, and seconds later, it was pushed completely from my grasp. I tumbled back, almost falling for a second time.

Ricky Moreno, The Jawbreaker, loomed large in the frame of my front door, reaching out a bloodied hand toward me.

"Help me."

Twelve

In my defence, the big human wasn't doing anything and hadn't been doing anything all day.

So sue me for wanting my warm bed to curl up in.

In retrospect it was a terrible idea but how was I to know?

--Thoughts from Loki

To my credit, I didn't scream.

Though it was less of a conscious act and more that I was in such a state of shock that I didn't even think about screaming. My brain focused on finding an escape route.

With Ricky blocking the door with his hulking frame, I was not getting out of the house that way. The back door was an option if I could outrun him. He was drunk and injured, so perhaps I had an advantage? A stab of pain in my head reminded me I wasn't in perfect health either. But I had to give it a shot.

The kitchen light was on, so I ran toward it like a moth to the flame. The primitive side of my brain equated the light to safety for some reason, although as soon as I stepped foot on the tile and my slipper slipped underneath me, I realised my mistake.

My hip slammed against the edge of the counter as my momentum carried me forwards too fast, pain biting into the skin all the way to the bone, my nerves vibrating like the door stopper Loki loved to play with.

Loki!

Hope flourished within me at the thought of my cats watching the scene with horror and coming to my aid. I didn't hear any vengeful yowls, but they would surely come charging any moment?

A glance at the corner of the room showed Loki still with his head in the bowl of treats.

Bloody cat.

"Help me!" Ricky repeated, staggering against the counter himself, though probably more because of the dangerous levels of alcohol in his blood than any issues with inappropriate footwear on polished tiles.

His hands left bloody smears wherever he grabbed, but his slow fumbling approach gave me time to right myself and make for the back door.

The key was hooked onto the wall beside it, but the keychain was full of keys. One key was the shed, one was my bike lock, one was a spare front door, and one would be the key I needed; the back door.

Of course, I got the wrong one the first time. Panic coursed through my veins and shot my heart rate up so I could feel my pulse in my wrists as my trembling hands fumbled with the ring of keys and selected another.

"Help, please," Ricky said.

Just as the key slotted into the lock, he reached me, his strong hands grabbing hold of the back of my nightshirt and then crushing me against his chest.

OK. Time to play his game. Not like I had a choice.

"Ricky? How can I help you, Ricky?" I asked, trying to push the panic down and keep my voice from trembling. My whole body was shaking now, any adrenaline had faded, and I was left with a horrible feeling of dread. That this was it. My luck had run out.

"You saw me. You saw I didn't do it," Ricky said. "You were there that morning. You saw I wasn't at the hotel."

To be honest, what I saw was him stumbling out of someone's hedge. Where he had been before that I hadn't a clue. But that answer probably wouldn't extend my life expectancy, so I lied. "Yes, I saw you. It wasn't you."

"Yeah, yeah," he agreed, bashing his chin against the top of my head with every nod. My head ached, and the alcohol on his breath was strong enough that I felt myself getting tipsy on the fumes.

"So if we agree, maybe let me go then?"

"No, no," he said, his thick, muscled arms pulling me tighter against his chest. "You need to tell the police. Tell them it wasn't me. Tell them to stop chasing me. Then I don't have to break their jaws."

"They'll be very pleased. And I would be more than happy to make a statement, but you're going to need to let me go so that I can go to the police station. If you walk me there like this, they'll arrest you on the spot for kidnap. It doesn't look good, manhandling a woman like this."

He was silent for a long moment. With my back pressed against his chest, I couldn't see the emotions playing out on his face, but I could feel his chest heaving in and out. He was panicked, terrified even. Or perhaps high on something. His bare arms were cold but damp with sweat.

Very, very slowly, I felt the pressure around me lessen as he relaxed his grip.

"I..." he began.

"Willow? Willow?" called a voice from the hallways.

Oh no. Bardot was home.

The arms around me tightened even further until I could no longer feel my feet on the ground. He lifted me bodily and transferred me to one arm, pinning me against him. The other hand reached for the kitchen island and the knife block.

"Thomas!" I screamed, not even thinking about using his first name.

The sting of the blade against my neck terrified me. But even without looking, I could feel he hadn't wounded me. He was just holding the kitchen knife to my skin, threatening Bardot not to take a step closer.

Bardot froze in the kitchen doorway, his face going grey as he took in the scene. I felt like a rag doll in Ricky's arm, but with the tight grip and the knife against my throat, I didn't see a way of getting myself free.

"Willow, are you alright?" Bardot asked, his hazel eyes fixed on mine.

"I'm– oww!" the knife bit a little closer, the cold metal of the blade scaring me more than I cared to admit and had me shivering in my nightie.

"She has something to say, don't you?" Ricky asked me, shaking me slightly as if I were a doll.

"He didn't do it. You've got the wrong man. Stop chasing him. Let him go free," I said. I didn't mind lying; I knew that Bardot would realise I was only saying it to get Ricky to let me go.

"There!" Ricky bellowed. "Now, your turn, policeman. Promise me I can go free. I did my time in prison. I was collecting what was mine. I didn't touch a hair on Georgie Weaver's damn head. It was my job to protect him. I just visited him, that's all. Nothing wrong with that."

"I can't make that promise, Ricky," Bardot said, his silky voice calm and even. Now his gaze was on Ricky. "I can promise you that you will be given a fair opportunity to provide a statement and tell your story. I can promise that you will not be under arrest, that I can take you to the station now, and we can go through your statement."

"I ain't going anywhere," He shifted me in his arms. The sheen of sweat on his skin glowed under the kitchen light. "I'm telling you now that I didn't do it. Isn't that enough?"

Bardot shook his head. Barely perceptibly, I could see him inching forward. "I'm afraid not, Ricky. I need it officially documented. I need you to tell me where you were that night, and I need to check your alibi."

"I told you I went to see him but didn't kill him. You're going to use that, aren't you? You'll pin this on me. You always do. Once a criminal, always a criminal, right? How the hell am I meant to break this cycle if you keep thinking I'm the bad guy?"

"You're holding a woman hostage at knifepoint in her own home," Bardot pointed out.

So good was Ricky's sob story that I'd almost started to feel sorry for him until I remembered that *I* was that woman.

"Put the knife down," Bardot said calmly. "And we'll talk."

"No. You'll lock me up is what you'll do."

Whatever Bardot may have said about that was lost in the chaos. Just as I noticed that Loki was no longer nibbling at his bowl, I heard the battle yowl I had been praying for five minutes earlier.

From seemingly nowhere, Loki attacked, leaping out of the wall and sinking his sharp fangs into Ricky's leg. It was a ballsy move, but then I supposed Loki hadn't realised that there was a risk Ricky could slice my throat open by accident.

Fortunately, Ricky's instinct was to drop the knife, which clattered to the floor. He hopped on one foot, yowling almost as loudly as Loki had, spinning as he hopped while searching for whatever had attacked him.

Of course, Loki had vanished, his heroic act completed. God, he was going to want a tonne of PsyTreats for that.

Bardot looked just as confused, probably because I'd told him that my cats were dead during my morphine-induced muzziness.

"I'll kill you all and that damn cat or rat or whatever the hell it was!" Ricky growled. He bent low, and just in time, I realised he was reaching for the knife. I leapt forward and kicked it out of reach. It spun off under the oven somewhere; I'd worry about that later.

Realising he was without a weapon, Ricky bolted. He slammed into the back door, not realising I hadn't had time to unlock it. That bought Bardot a couple of seconds but not quite enough to stop Ricky from leaving.

The two of them raced out into the night. I watched from the side kitchen window as Ricky instinctively ran for the trees that bordered my little home and the luxurious mansion of Woodburton Hall next door.

The woods were massive and easy to lose your way in, especially at night. Hurriedly I dug a torch from the junk drawer in the kitchen and grabbed my coat, awkwardly threading my arms into sleeves as I left the warmth of the house and entered the chill of the woods.

A fine misty rain fell, and I could feel my hair frizzing. My coat shone in the moonlight from the rain, and I swung the torch beam around desperately, searching for traces of where they had gone.

"Oww!"

I ran toward the voice, my heart thumping in my chest so painfully it felt as if my heart had ballooned to ten times its usual size. It was hard to force my lungs to breathe as I ran, stumbling in my slippers on tree roots, the torch beam bouncing and swaying in time with my jogging.

Soon the white light found a dark lump on the ground. Bardot blinked up at me, his face pale in the direct light.

"Not the eyes," he groaned.

"Sorry," I swung the light down to the hedge he had fallen into. Or rather... "Oh no!"

"Yeah, I thought they were stinging nettles," he said with a heavy sigh, picking the prickly green plants from his dark uniform. "I fell right in, lucky my hands braced my impact so I didn't fall face first. Ricky got away."

"It's fine. It's fine. So long as you're ok," I said, my heart rate lowering from a million to nine hundred and ninety-nine thousand beats per minute.

"Me? Course. What about you? Did he hurt you?" Bardot got to his feet, wincing and rubbing at his palms.

"I'm ok. I will be, anyway. I just need to calm down. That was insane."

"Yeah, it was," he said, standing in front of me, watching me in the torch's light. Long shadows played on his face, giving him the hooded angular look of a villain. A very hot villain.

"Thank you. For saving me," I said.

"It's nothing. Quick thinking kicking the knife away. Otherwise, this might have been a much less happy ending."

"Yeah, well," I shrugged but warmed at the compliment. I had helped. Maybe even saved Bardot.

"The cat..." he said, tipping his head quizzically.

I closed my eyes and shook my head. I ached. I was exhausted. "I'll explain later."

"Right," he said. "We should get back. You're frozen."

He reached out a hand to my shoulder, warming the skin where he touched.

Neither of us made any attempt to go home.

Perhaps it was the adrenaline running in our bodies. Maybe it was the shared near-death experience and that we had saved one another. But we both felt it, I was sure. That our relationship had stepped over a threshold. We had bonded with a red thread of fate, tying us to one another.

He leaned down; I tilted my head up. Our lips met in a warm, passionate kiss as our bodies came together. Hands grabbed, we pulled each other close, needing to feel, to taste, to smell the other. To know that they were ok. That nothing bad had happened.

When we parted, his hazel eyes were bright, his lips a beautiful deep pink.

"We should..." he said.

"We should," I agreed.

And we did. We walked home. Hand in hand.

Thirteen

Of course I went chasing with the detective. There was a thrill to the hunt as we raced through the darkness, moonlight guiding us as we pursued the criminal. I already had the tang of blood on my fangs and I was ready for action.

Until the human stumbled and I was so surprised I stopped myself to check on him. My own human would be most displeased if he had died. But he was fine, he had simply fallen into nettles.

But by then I'd lost the scent and the big brutish human was gone.

Typical.

--Thoughts from Loki

We weren't holding hands the next day.

Bardot wasn't holding much of anything.

"Oww. Dammit. Oww. Dammit." He repeated, over and over, as he gingerly lifted a cup of tea to his lips but had to set it down when the cup was too much for his poor blistered skin.

"We should have found the dock leaves," I mused sadly, sipping my own tea and feeling rather guilty. "There's always dock leaves next to stinging nettles."

"Dock leaves?" Bardot asked, confusion and pain sharpening his voice.

"City boy," I chided. "You rub dock leaves on stinging nettle rashes. For some reason, nature grows them in pairs, so you have the stinger and antidote next to each other. I didn't even think about it last night."

"We were a little preoccupied," Bardot admitted. "I remember something in scouts about dock leaves. Suppose it's too late now."

"I'd say so; your hands look awful. They're a good natural remedy but not a miracle cure."

The skin on his hands was bright red, pocked with dozens of pale raised bumps scattered like stars in the sky. The itching was driving him crazy, and he kept rubbing his hands on his trousers, the woven seat cover of the kitchen chair and anything abrasive to offer some relief. I even caught him biting his fingers to counteract the itching with pain.

"Stop scratching," I said, catching him in the act.

"I can't. I just *can't*," he groaned. "This is horrible."

"You need some antihistamine cream. And some chamomile lotion. Then you'll be right as rain."

"Hurricane or a storm, maybe," he grumbled, making another attempt at lifting the mug to his lips with his swollen mitts.

"You really are grumpy when you're not well. Duly noted."

"For the future?" he asked, a hint of hope edging his words.

"For the future," I agreed, offering him a smile that melted some of the frown creases from his face.

While Bardot was distracted with itching and tea, I casually scrolled on my tablet. The local news archives were helpful as I searched Georgie Weaver's name and then his cell block, hoping for some hints about his relationship with The Jawbreaker.

Bingo. Two years ago, there was an incident at cell block B-2 where a man named Skull Crusher (what was it with these violent nicknames?) had fractured the skull of a prison guard. At least he was on brand.

A write-up of the incident included a couple of accomplices, including someone named The Jawbreaker. Bingo. Their real names were listed as Greg Hollow and Richard Moreno, so I felt reasonably safe with my research. Now I had a name, a contact that might be able to help shed some light on Jawbreaker's relationship with Georgie and how he might fit a murder profile.

Feeling smug, I discreetly switched to a cat video and set the tablet flat on the table just as Bardot hissed in pain again as he lifted the cup to his lips. He managed two sips of tea before his hands stung so badly that he nearly dropped the cup. Instantly he began alternating scratching each hand, then found a happy nirvana where he cupped his hands and scratched both simultaneously.

"You're going to end up bleeding," I warned.

"I don't care."

"Or scarred for life."

"I still don't care. This is heavenly."

From the corner of my eye, I saw Luna appear through the door, walking through it as if it were a sheet of gossamer rather than a wooden structure. She paused, glancing around the kitchen, her keen blue eyes training on her bowl. Her empty bowl. She turned to me with large round eyes looking for all the world as if I'd stolen her firstborn.

"Mow?" she asked, confused. Translated as: *Breakfast?*

My breath caught in my lungs, and I rose to my feet before I knew what I was doing. Bardot couldn't hear her, but how long would she stay not-solid if I didn't give her treats? Bardot would freak out if she turned corporeal and started moving things in the middle of the kitchen.

"I'll go check again if I have any antihistamine," I said quickly.

Bardot blinked from where he was furiously attacking the blisters with his neatly clipped nails. "I thought you said you didn't have any?"

"I just remembered another place I might keep it. Let me go check."

I hurried out of the room, hoping that Luna would follow me. She did, her ghostly paws skimming the carpet as we raced upstairs. Pretending to bang around in the medicine cabinet, I lowered my voice for her.

"Sorry, Luna. I promise you will get treats later. Double the amount. But right now, I can't, not with him sitting there. He doesn't know about you. I told him you were dead."

"Mow?" she asked, her ears turning slightly and her head tipping.

I sighed. "Yes, I know you are dead. But generally, humans think that when someone is dead, they can't be seen again. I know differently. You know differently. But before we introduce you, let me warm him up and talk to him first, ok? Please, Luna?"

She looked unconvinced.

I leaned closer to her, lowering my voice even more. Girl-to-girl talk. "Look, Luna. I really like him. It's early days, but I think we could have something really special. So I need you to keep out of sight for now. I promise you double treats when we're alone again."

She still looked unconvinced.

"Ok, triple."

"Mow." *Deal*.

"Thank you."

I crept down the stairs and plastered on a grin as I joined Bardot in the kitchen.

"Still no antihistamine?" Bardot asked. He was halfway through with his cup of tea.

"No, sorry. I thought maybe there was some behind the sun cream, but no."

Bardot nodded. Once. Twice. Then: "Your cat bowl moved."

"My what?"

"Cat bowl. In the corner. It moved. On its own."

"The cat bowl. Oh, that cat bowl!" I looked at the two little metal bowls set out for Luna and Loki. Luna, I had pacified. Loki was there now, glaring at me. Clearly, he had caused a fuss and kicked his bowl to get attention.

"Yes, that cat bowl. Are there others?"

"Well, no. Those are the only cat bowls I have. For the cats I had."

"The ones that died," Bardot said.

"Yes, the ones that died," I said. "They are most certainly dead." At least that wasn't a lie.

Starting to feel like I was under interrogation, I headed to the front door, unhooked my coat from the rack, and began jamming my feet into my sneakers.

"Why don't we get an early start on the pharmacy? I assume you're going in to work, but you really will scratch your skin off if you don't do something about that first."

"I haven't got time. I need to–"

"You've got time. It'll only take a minute, and it's hardly far. Nothing in Catton Strawless is very far. Take a few minutes now to get some stuff to help, and you'll work much better if you're not driving yourself mad itching."

His mouth opened to protest. I imagined Mr Perfect Police Officer had never been late for work in his life. Or taken even five minutes off. Or been thirty seconds late on a lunch break.

So it was a testament to how sore his hands were that he sighed heavily and hung his head. "Fine. Let's go."

I pushed open the pharmacy door as it looked like Bardot might struggle. I had no idea how he intended to drive, take notes, use a computer, or even go to the loo. But he was stubborn as hell. He must be a Taurus. I'd have to ask him sometime.

"Hello and good morning," said a man with a large moustache curled at the tips.

"Hi, Charlie," I said. Charlie was the pharmacy's owner and had been here for as long as I could remember.

A childhood memory of my aunt carrying me here when I was young as I bawled my eyes out because I'd scraped my knee. I remembered kind Charlie taking a plaster from a multipack and making a big show of dressing it properly. Then he plucked a lolly from the tub on the counter and gave it to me free of charge for "being a brave patient".

The lollipops were gone now, replaced with a stand full of flavoured lip balms. Now the idea was planted in my head I wanted a lolly.

"Oh dear me, I don't think I need to ask why you're here," Charlie said, his trained eyes zeroing in on Bardot's hands, which were nuclear red and seemingly double their usual size. "What happened, lad?"

"I was in pursuit of a person of interest and had a minor mishap with some native foliage."

Charlie raised a bushy grey eyebrow and glanced at me.

"He was running and tripped into some stinging nettles," I translated.

"Aha, yes, they can leave a nasty rash. Looks like perhaps you've not been kind to your skin. Have you been scratching them?" Charlie asked.

"Not much," Bardot said.

"Tonnes," I translated.

"Uh huh," Charlie said, then turned to the shelves behind him and plucked a box of antihistamine cream from the shelf. He set it down on the glass counter and rung up the charge. "Seven ninety-nine for instant relief."

"Done," Bardot said, swiping his phone to pay and opening the box right away to start smoothing the cream over his poor palms.

"Since you're here," Charlie said, trying to act casual but with the tone of someone who was finally getting around to admitting the embarrassing reason they wanted to talk to you in the first place. "I wondered if you could give me some advice."

"Me or him?" I asked.

"Him. Unless you've brushed up on police procedure?"

"I caught a murderer," I pointed out.

"So you did. But my problem is hopefully a far cry from murder. See, we have a locked cupboard where we keep the controlled medicines. You know, the ones we really need to keep an eye on, the strong painkillers and that kind of thing."

"Right," Bardot said, half listening as he smothered his hands in the white paste. It didn't seem to want to absorb into his skin, probably because he had used half a tube.

"Well, I do an audit every week. A stock check to make sure everything that should be in the cupboard is in the cupboard. It's good practice. You have to do it for the regulators, you see?"

"I see," Bardot said, still fighting a losing battle rubbing the cream in.

"Well, yesterday was audit day. So I went through everything, checked it against our records, and found something missing."

Bardot's head snapped up. Police mode activated. "Missing? What was missing?"

"A strong painkiller. Only one bottle, mind you. But a very high concentration." Charlie shook his head, set his gnarled hands on the counter and rested his weight against them. "Now, it could have been an honest error, perhaps someone booked them in wrong, and we never had the bottle in the first place."

"But you don't think so?" Bardot pressed.

Charlie shook his head, pressing his lips together tightly.

"What makes you suspect foul play?"

"The bottle was in my stock take last week. I checked through our electronic records to see if any had been issued, but as I said, it's pretty strong stuff; we don't prescribe it often. Only keep it on hand in case someone needs it urgently for an end of life patient."

"So it was there, and now it's not?" Bardot said.

"Right. So either someone broke the vial and hasn't owned up, accidentally gave out the medicine and didn't realise, or they stole it. To use, to sell, who knows."

Bardot nodded. "I'm sure you have procedures for this?"

"I do. But I just wanted an off the record conversation first. Because I know it wasn't me, but I only have a few staff, and I trust them with my life."

"You know what you have to do. Report it officially to your regulator. If someone has intentionally taken a controlled drug, that's not something you can overlook."

Charlie's shoulders slumped, and he looked every one of his sixty-odd years. "You're right. Thank you."

Bardot nodded, and I swear he'd have tipped his hat if he was wearing one and said, "Just doing my job".

As he turned to leave, I had one more question. My curiosity couldn't leave it unasked. "What was the drug, out of interest?"

"Oh? Injectable Morphine. Twenty milligrams per one millilitre."

"Thanks," I said. "And thanks for the antihistamine. Have a good day."

"You too," Charlie called, his face dark as he prepared to call in that one of his controlled drugs had gone walkabout.

As soon as I stepped outside, I nearly walked into Bardot, who had frozen in place.

"He said morphine, didn't he?" Bardot asked.

"Yeah. Strong morphine."

"I need to go. I'll be back tonight."

"Ok," I said, but he had already hurried off, his long legs setting a brisk pace to wherever he needed to be.

For a moment, I pondered what could have set off an idea in his mind. I felt close to a revelation when my own brain jerked to life, and a stab of panic ran through me like lightning down a rod. "Pippa!"

I jogged home as fast as I could, hoping I hadn't kept her waiting for our prison date.

Fourteen

While of course I am not happy that the detective was hurt, it was hardly a life-threatening injury. The best part was that it gave Willow a chance to tend to him, to touch his hands and to look after him.

Very sweet and hopefully the detective has now seen a caring, concerned side to our wonderful Willow. I tried to talk to Loki about it but he pretended to start coughing up a hairball.

--Thoughts from Luna

Pippa's blue Ford was idling outside my front door. As I approached from behind, I caught a glimpse of Pippa pressing up against the glass of her window, then reaching out to honk her horn.

She did a fabulous impression of someone thrown out of a car using an ejector seat when I rapped my knuckles on the passenger side window.

"Darling, that was not funny," she said, her hand pressed against her chest and her eyes briefly closing. "Could have given me a heart attack, and then who would have driven you to prison?"

"That's a good point. Also, I would miss an awesome, excellent friend if you died."

"Who said I would die? Heart attacks aren't always fatal," she said, easing us onto the road as I clipped in my seat belt.

We were silent for barely a second before she began her interrogation.

"Where were you this early?"

"Pharmacy."

"Again? You needed more painkillers? Are you taking the right amount? You should still have enough."

"Not for me. Thomas stayed over last night; long story short, he needed to get a rash seen to this morning."

Too late, I realised that my attempts at being vague and putting her off follow-up questions made the whole thing sound a hundred times worse and would lead to much more questioning.

I didn't realise that I would shock her so much that she made a strange, animal-like sound, turned to me, spun the steering wheel the other way and ended up braking hard just before we nosedived into a ditch.

For a second, we both sat in our seats, hearts racing and breathing laboured as we stared down the fall ahead of us, which could trap us in the vehicle and drown us in one fell swoop.

"I don't even know where to start," Pippa said, obviously still more flustered by my words than our near-death experience.

At least the country lane had been empty of traffic.

"How about you start with getting us away from this ditch? Preferably before the grass sinks and we slide in and get trapped?" I asked, my nerves slightly frayed, thinking about how close to the edge of the ditch the wheels must be.

"Right, right," Pippa distractedly backed us up, waiting for a lone tractor to pass, then reversed onto the road and recommenced our journey.

"Oh my god," I said, my hand resting on the door of the car, perhaps subconsciously worried that I might need to bail out at a moment's notice.

"I know," Pippa said, shaking her head. "What did you give him? And when did he become Thomas? And why is he staying over?"

Of course, Pippa recovered quickly from the accident and again focused on the gossip. I tried to relax my body, but every muscle felt as if it had been wound up tight like a clockwork mouse toy.

"I didn't give him anything! He fell into some stinging nettles."

"Seriously, that is the *worst* excuse I've ever heard. And I've heard a lot of excuses."

"The rash is on his hands," I insisted. "Not down there."

"Huh. Well, maybe if he was–"

"Do not go there!" I snapped, blushing as hot as the sun. "We did nothing. He's staying in the spare room. The last time there was a murder, he had to keep going back home to North

Walsham, which was ridiculous. So I offered him a room to crash in when he's working late."

"Right. Fine."

"It's true!"

"Ok. But where do the stinging nettles come in?"

"He was helping with some gardening as a thank you, and he grabbed a big clump and didn't realise what they were until it was too late."

Pippa's lips pursed. Her eyes narrowed, but she mercifully kept her gaze forward. As we got closer to Norwich, the traffic increased, and I didn't think we'd be so lucky if she spun us off the road again now.

"I'll get the truth from you one day," Pippa said.

I sighed but relaxed. She was dropping it, and that was good. The last thing I needed was to explain I'd let a murder suspect into my home and was held at knifepoint. The tiny cut on my neck still stung if I bent my head the wrong way, but it was nearly invisible, so I hadn't bothered to hide it with a scarf.

Fortunately, Pippa had forgotten about my calling Bardot by his first name. It was slipping out more and more these days, and it felt right. Why I had insisted on calling him by his surname from the beginning, I didn't know. Unless it was an unconscious attempt to distance myself, knowing that I found him attractive, but with his aloof attitude it felt like he was untouchable.

Except he wasn't. Not really. He was human. He could smile. He could laugh. And he had looked very, humanly terrified when he had seen the knife pressed against my throat.

Norwich is an urban haven within Norfolk's large, otherwise mostly rural, county. It has a prominent high street with all the popular shops like fashion chains and expensive restaurants fronted by famous restaurants. It has theatres, cinemas, a roller rink and even a medieval castle dating back to the twelfth century.

It also houses a prison for category B and C male offenders. To us laypeople, that's those who are not a genuine flight risk and haven't actively murdered someone. The bad but not-as-bad-as-they-could-be prisoners.

After exiting the main dual carriageway, we snaked through some residential streets and then onto a narrow part council-owned road that wound long and thin past a few newly built houses and a charming little pale green pub. On the left, trees loomed tall and foreboding, blotting out the sun and chilling the air.

We passed two car parks following the signs for visitors and eventually parked in a small lot outside a magnificent red-bricked building, alongside a handful of other cars. One was an electric blue Subaru with a spoiler taller than I was. Stickers adorned the rear bumper and window, including one with a stick figure humping the word "it". It took me a moment to understand, and then I couldn't decide whether to laugh or roll my eyes.

"Reception is that way," Pippa nodded to the signed wooden door.

Disorientated by the number of buildings and doors and signs, I hurried after Pippa so as not to get lost. Inside smelt sterile and airless. A receptionist sat behind plexiglass.

"Can I help you?" she asked finally.

"Yes, please, we're here to visit someone," I said sweetly.

"Well, this *is* the visiting area, so I can't say I'm shocked. Name?"

Wow. Rude. "Willow Addison. But you see–"

She tapped something and squinted at her screen. "Who are you here to see?"

"Skull Crusher. Or maybe you have him under Greg Hollow."

She tutted in a way that screamed, "what do you think?" and tapped away at her computer before frowning.

"Have you booked an appointment?" she asked, her gaze travelling at the speed of a glacier from the screen to my face.

"No, see, I was trying to explain before you cut me off that–"

"If you haven't rung ahead, I can't do anything. Prison policy." She sat back in her chair, wrapping skinny arms around her chest and looking all the world like she had just beaten me at a game of chess or something.

Well, the joke was on her. I was pretty damn good at chess. And really bad at knowing when I was beaten.

"Can I make an appointment now, *please?*" I asked, emphasising the last word so she would know I didn't mean it.

"I'm *so* sorry. But prison policy requires requests to be booked in advance."

Oh, she was good. Using the same technique back at me, saying all the right polite words but with a threatening undertone that warned me against messing with her.

Hah, as if I'd take notice of that.

Still smiling wide and fake, I held out my hand to Pippa. "Phone, please."

Without a word, Pippa handed me her phone. I quickly googled the prison's number for the visitor wing. The receptionist's smile was fading, her eyes filling with hatred and trying to burn me with her glare.

The phone on her desk rang. We continued our staring match as she reached for it and held the receiver to her ear.

"Good morning, Norwich Prison Visitors Wing. How can I help you?"

Her voice echoed in my ear, out of sync with the real-life version in front of me.

"I'd like to book a visit, please."

"What was your name?" she asked, her phone voice very efficient and polite. I had the feeling these calls may be recorded. And no matter how livid she was at me, she didn't want to risk an unblemished customer service record.

"Willow Addison."

"Thank you. Who would you like to visit, please?"

"Greg Hollow, AKA Skull Crusher."

"Hold, please."

The receptionist pressed a button on the phone. Music blared so loudly that the little hairs in my ear stood on end. The smirk on her red lips told me she was in control of the volume of the hold music.

While I held the phone away from my ear to avoid premature hearing loss, the receptionist dialled internally and spoke to someone within the prison.

"Yeah, the stupid woman won't leave until she's seen him. Don't think she's on his visitors list. Can you check with him?" The receptionist flashed me a fake smile.

Clearly, the internal lines were not recorded for training and monitoring purposes.

She kept me on hold for a long while, even after I could see that she had finished. She just sat there, watching me, until finally, she was bored enough to take me off hold.

"So sorry to keep you. Greg Hollow is enjoying his exercise hour but will be finished shortly and is willing to add you to his visitors list. Are you happy to wait?"

"That would be fine. Thank you so much for your help."

"You are more than welcome, have a lovely day."

She hung up. I swiped to end the call.

"Tart," she said with a saccharine smile.

"Cow," I returned with a smile of my own.

"Take a seat. I'm sure he won't be *too* long."

She sounded far too happy about that. *Far* too happy.

I wish I'd brought something to read.

Fifteen

God bless Pippa. I'm sure if she could see me, we'd be great friends. Both of us want the same thing: Willow and the detective together. Not being able to communicate has its disadvantages. One day I'll have to try out touching Pippa, see how she reacts to an invisible feline.

Maybe Willow will explain to her? Or to the detective? Suppose he ever were to live with us, Willow would have a lot of questions to answer.

I do sometimes wish she'd tell others but I appreciate it's a bit of a leap of faith for others to believe when they can't see us. I'll know it's serious if she ever tells the detective.

--Thoughts from Luna

We waited for over an hour.

Unless recreation hour had just begun when we arrived, we were being kept waiting on purpose. I got the feeling the receptionist had something to do with it. She typed furiously and constantly but would pause every so often to look over her screen at us and smirk.

My brain conjured images of her instant messaging colleagues to tell them, "just another fifteen minutes".

With nothing to occupy it, my mind wandered. Pippa seemed content in reading and re-reading the few posters on the wall that implored the public to be vigilant and call the non-emergency police line 101 if they had any concerns.

A neat A4 sheet of paper was also tacked to the wall, listing visitor conduct when meeting with prisoners. I couldn't be bothered to read them, but I made up my own set of rules in my head. Surely they didn't need to be that long? Number one – don't help the prisoner escape. Kind of covered everything, didn't it?

While spending the time crossing and uncrossing my legs out of sheer boredom, I wondered how Thomas was doing. Then my brain switched gears and posed the question Pippa had forgotten about earlier: when had he switched from Bardot to Thomas?

The answer was blurred. It had been creeping in slowly. Yet it seemed to happen all at once too. Last night. The kiss. We hadn't spoken about it, but it meant something. A barrier around his heart had been breached, a tiny hole that let a shard of light through. More demolition work was needed, but I could see fragments of hope for us.

I think I had almost dozed off when the receptionist finally spoke, startling me to my senses.

"Skull Crusher will see you now."

I was sure she had used his nickname to intimidate me, but the joke was on her. I had already been intimidated by The Jawbreaker. I was desensitised to steroid-abuse thugs with ridiculous made-up names.

A few minutes later, we were sitting in what looked like my old high school cafeteria. Several tables with groups of bright blue plastic chairs clumped around them. By the door was an older couple, hunched across the table, speaking in hushed tones to one another. In the far corner by the window, a younger man and woman were also leaning across the table but were quite passionately making out. A guard was already on his way over to break them up but bless them they were determined to make every last second count.

The only other occupied table contained a man in a grey t-shirt and sweatpants, watching us intently as we entered the room. I assumed this was Skull Crusher. The fact that he had an actual skull tattooed on his face was a) a good indication and b) very distracting. His shaven head added the haunting image.

My chest constricted with fear as I approached, and my legs turned to jelly. Ok, maybe this was a bit different to my encounters with The Jawbreaker; this time, I had to force myself to move toward the danger.

His eyes were such a dark brown that they were almost black, giving the skull on his face a hollowed-eyed look as he carefully watched me approach.

"Hello. Thank you for meeting us, Mr Crusher," I stuttered, almost fumbling as I reached for a chair and sat down opposite him.

For a moment, I wondered if he would crush my skull. His stare was intense, his frame large and strong like Ricky Moreno's. I had to reassure myself that this was not a maximum security prison and that the people here had not committed the most heinous crimes. But damn, did he look capable.

He leaned forward a little, and I could smell chilli on his breath. My heart skipped a beat. I thought I might faint from fear.

"No probs, sweetheart. Call me Greg. I don't really go by Skull Crusher anymore. It was fun for a while, but as you get a bit older, you start to have different priorities, you know?"

His voice was strangely soft and high-pitched. His skull tattoo deformed as he smiled brightly at us.

My body deflated like a popped balloon, and my confidence returned in bucketloads.

"Thanks, Greg," I said as the last of the adrenaline faded from my body, and I could function as a normal human again. "I'm Willow, and this is Pippa."

"Lovely to meet you. How can I help?" Greg asked.

"We were hoping you could tell us a bit about Ricky Moreno. Maybe you know him as The Jawbreaker?" I said, scanning his face for recognition. The sockets around his eyes creased in thought. "He was released a few weeks ago. He was probably friendly with Georgie Weaver?"

"I know who you mean, sweetheart," Greg said, nodding to himself. "There was someone who did like going by his nickname. He took a lot of pride in his reputation did The Jawbreaker."

Optimism stirred within me. I sat up straighter. "Do you know what his relationship was with Georgie? Any reason why he might try to contact him outside of prison? Maybe something to do with money?"

"Oh yeah, I can definitely help you out there," Greg said, rolling his shoulders as if preparing for a bout of boxing instead of a conversation. "See, lots of the lads here take on odd jobs. Most of them are official. Did you know we can learn new trades? You can work in the kitchen or laundry. Breaks the day up, you know? And earns you a bit of pocket money."

"Right. So The Jawbreaker did laundry for Georgie?" I asked, trying to understand where this was going.

Greg laughed, a bold laugh as big as he was. "God, no. He wouldn't have touched work like that. Nah, The Jawbreaker took on some unofficial work, if you know what I mean? A few ways to make a different sort of money in here. Risky. But some of the guys live off the adrenaline."

"Ok. So what did he do?" I leaned forward, desperate to find out what kind of things were going on here.

"A few of the guys are in the import business. By that I mean smuggling. But the other line of work is personal security. The Jawbreaker was more into that. Have you ever met him? Even in prison, he's not someone you'd want to get on the wrong side of. So the perfect hire if you want to keep people away."

"Like a bodyguard?" I asked.

Greg made a clicking sound and pointed a finger at me like a gun. Not going to lie; that looked kind of scary. "You got it, sweetheart. Georgie was worried, you see. He was getting old, sick, and not really able to intimidate the younger guys like he used to. So he employed The Jawbreaker to stick around and warn other people off him. Give him breathing room so he wasn't harassed. Lots of people around here know someone he screwed over, so Georgie was always getting flack. Nasty words you can live with, but in the yard, it's nice to have a friendly set of fists. Even if they're hired."

"So why would The Jawbreaker come to Georgie now?"

"Easy." Greg leaned back in his chair, his massive arms folded across his chest. "Payment time. Georgie didn't have money in prison. The Jawbreaker couldn't use money in prison. The deal would have been based on a gentleman's agreement, with the work done up front, and then The Jawbreaker would have gotten his money when released."

"Except he didn't," I said, realisation dawning on me like a lightbulb illuminating the answer. "Georgie performed one last scam. He didn't pay The Jawbreaker for the work."

"Well, if he skipped payment, then I can't say what would happen," Greg said, shaking his head. "The Jawbreaker was famous for his temper. He was a short fuse, didn't get that nickname for nothing, you know?"

"Oh, I know. I read the news reports on him," I said. "So you think if he found out he'd been tricked, he would be angry?"

"Angry?" Greg said, laughing that loud, bellow of a laugh. "He'd bloody kill Georgie!"

Perhaps the look on my face said it all. Greg immediately stopped laughing, unfolded his arms and leaned across the table, concern under that tattoo mask.

"Georgie's dead?"

I nodded silently.

"Damn. Well, there's your man. If The Jawbreaker had thought he'd been tricked, it wouldn't have been just about the money. His pride would have driven him to murder too."

I turned this over in my head. It painted an obvious picture. Almost too obvious. I couldn't quite match it with the image of The Jawbreaker in my home, holding me hostage, begging me to tell the police he didn't do it. All of his actions were very raw, brutal. Yet Georgie's murder was more delicate. Not The Jawbreaker's style.

"Out of interest, if The Jawbreaker were to kill Georgie, how would he do it?"

Greg snorted, the arms folded across his chest again. "Well, he'd start by breaking his jaw. Then every other bone in his body, one by one."

Of course.

"Thanks, Greg."

"Anytime, sweetheart."

Pippa and I returned to the car and sat silently for a long moment.

"They're looking for him now, right?" Pippa asked. "The police are on the hunt for The Jawbreaker?"

"Yeah, they'll catch up with him, I'm sure. He's not the sharpest claw on the paw and has no resources. Sooner or later, they'll find him and question him."

"But you don't think they'll get what they need."

I turned to Pippa. "What makes you say that?"

"I know you. You don't like this."

"No. You heard Greg. If The Jawbreaker had done it, the room would have been a bloodbath. Georgie's body would have been beaten to a pulp. Yet there wasn't a mark on his body. He died from a morphine overdose."

"How did you—"

"Thomas told me. Don't tell anyone," I said dismissively. "But can you see someone like The Jawbreaker taking the time to load up an injection of morphine and kill someone that way? The hotel room next door heard an argument. The Jawbreaker was drunk. If he were going to kill Georgie, he'd have used fists, not medication. It just doesn't fit."

"Have to say it doesn't sound like it fits. But what other explanation is there? Other than..."

She trailed off. I sighed deeply.

It made sense. Isaac was weak and would have to kill him subtly. It all fit, apart from the motive. But maybe Georgie wasn't going to pay him either, and it drove him over the edge?

"Isaac." We both said together.

Sixteen

The weedy giraffe-lookalike man? A killer? Certainly not. Once again the police here are making a mockery of their good name.

I admit that if it was the nurse, then a fatal injection would be the best method for him. With those stringy arms brute force would be out of the question. Despite his age and illness, the ex-convict had still been strong. And far more confident.

Still, I think it's a bit far-fetched. The human wouldn't say boo to a ghost. He'd just faint. But then I've seen stranger things.

--Thoughts from Loki

Pippa brought me to the café, and I did a light day's work of helping out with drinks in between idly browsing the adoption websites for new cats. The perfect ones were out there. I knew it. I just needed to be patient.

We had agreed on an extra three-month lease, and Thomas offered to pay the rent costs plus the rebrand. I had no idea where he was getting the money from, but I didn't want to abuse his goodwill by taking too long to do the redesign.

Fortunately, business had been good the last week because of the Georgie media circus, but that was already dying down. The journalists had switched to hounding Bardot by telephone, no longer needing to be at the crime scene now that the body had been removed and the crime scene techs were gone.

Last I heard, the room was still locked up in case anything further was needed, but the hotel was running as usual. Even the protestors on the grass had packed up and left.

"Wonder what happened to everyone," I mused, during a slow period without a single customer and with rain gently pattering against the large window.

"Everyone?" Pippa asked, her voice slightly dreamy as if she had been lost in her thoughts.

I wondered what she was thinking about. But I got in first, so I continued.

"The people and families who lost their money and camped outside the hotel. I wonder what they're doing now."

We sat on a counter, one not used for preparing food, with our legs dangling free. Pippa's yellow pumps kicked her heels against the cupboard door beneath us.

"Gone home, I guess? What's the point in protesting against someone who's dead? Not going to get their money now, are they?"

"I don't think it was ever about money. Well, maybe a bit. I think some were curious. To see the man that had left such a deep scar on their lives."

"Or throw rotten fruit at him."

"Or that," I agreed.

"Maybe you're right. I think people were there for all sorts of reasons. The ones that were properly angry, like the fruit guy I get. He wanted to make Georgie feel bad or hurt for what he did. He was trying to get justice. But what about the ones that were just *there*. No real reason, just...there. Like that woman with the hood."

"Woman with the hood?" I asked.

Honestly, I'd been to the hotel more times than my fair share. Far more times than anybody had any right to pass casually. It's not like the hotel was even on my route to work, I had to make a detour, yet I had passed it many times. And racking my brain, I could not remember a woman with a hood. Although it stood to reason that somebody could have put a jacket hood up, it hadn't rained recently. Today was the first day I could remember in a long time.

Pippa tapped a finger against her cheek as she thought. "Yeah, she just stood at the back and watched. I didn't get a good look at her. But I did see some hair peeking out, a tropical watery blue. I was thinking of re-dying mine. I've been purple for so long that I fancy something new. What do you think of blue? Or red?"

"Either would look great. But I've got used to your purple. It suits you."

Pippa smiled and nudged me gently with her shoulder. "You're sweet. Speaking of sweet..."

Her gaze had fixed out of the large window. Rain pelted down now, but the blurry figure making his way to the door was unmistakable.

"Hi there, business or pleasure?" Pippa asked, sliding off the counter and ready to make drinks if we needed them,

"Respite. Refuelling." Thomas sank into a chair and itched idly at his hands. Time to reapply the antihistamine cream by the looks of it.

"Flat white coming up," Pippa said, winking at me as a sign to go talk to him.

I didn't need to be told twice.

"Found The Jawbreaker yet?"

Bardot shook his head, drumming blistered fingers against the tabletop. "A few leads, but he seems to vanish before we can get there. He'll make a mistake soon enough."

I was about to tell him about my trip to the prison and what I'd learned when he continued. Which was unusual for him; he wasn't the type to confide unless I nagged. Lots.

"I might be doing better catching the potential suspect if I wasn't drowning in paperwork."

"Oh?"

"Claims. Solicitors. Everybody in Catton Strawless and their uncle seems to have banded together to sue for some of Georgie's estate and now there are dozens of freedom of information requests."

"What estate? Surely everything he had was repossessed when he went down?"

"Seems that a few weeks ago, his dear great aunt in Cork popped her clogs. Pardon the pun. She left him a cool five million. Someone found out, and now everyone who ever so much as lent him a tenner wants a slice of the pie."

"Yikes. That sounds like a headache." Internally I was wondering how I could claim myself, thinking of the money my aunt had lost to Georgie.

"Headache? I'm trying to catch a murderer at large, and people are worried about the money they lost decades ago."

"It's the principle of the matter, too," I pointed out, feeling guilty for thinking about my aunt's money.

The coffee arrived, a large mug for Thomas and a tall latte for me.

"Thanks, Pippa."

"Anytime." She grabbed a chair and sat with us.

"And to make matters worse, we're going to the press tomorrow with the post-mortem results, and we can't rule out that the morphine overdose was given on purpose."

Thomas rested his elbows on the table and ran his hands through his hair, then seemed to think better of it when that stung his skin. He grimaced and scratched. There were nail marks and lanes of raw skin.

"Put more cream on," I chided.

He grumbled but plucked the tube from his pocket and rubbed some between his palms.

"What's happening with Isaac?" I asked.

"Kid's been released. I just questioned him but haven't got a reason to hold him. He's the most likely suspect based on the method. It's a bit of a sneaky cowardly MO that I could see him doing. The kid isn't physically imposing, and it sounds like he was terrified of Georgie."

"Yeah, he would jump any time his phone rang," Pippa agreed.

"The Jawbreaker was there that night. Prints on the smashed bottle prove it was his. Likely he was the person the next room heard arguing with Georgie. But an argument and a smashed bottle don't make a murderer. And Ricky wouldn't have thought about the morphine. If it were a crime of passion, he would have used fists. And what made him angry enough to kill?"

I nodded enthusiastically, keen to add what I had learned. "Exactly. Thomas, today we–"

"Sorry," he interrupted me as his phone vibrated. He dug it out of another pocket and swiped to answer. "Bardot. Uhuh. Yeah. Uhuh. Are you sure? Uhuh. Ok. Call me if you find anything else."

"You say uhuh a lot," I pointed out as he hung up.

"It covers for what I really want to say."

"Which is?"

"Right now, words that are not suitable for polite company."

"I can't imagine you swearing," I said, feeling my cheeks burn as I imagined all the dirty words I could think of emerging from his lips. "What was the problem?"

"No problem."

"I'll ask again, what's the problem?"

He shook his head. "Police business."

"I heard the word morphine. And you looked more grumpy. So something is wrong with the morphine."

"I looked 'more' grumpy? Does that mean I always look grumpy?"

"Yes. Now stop avoiding the question. What's wrong with the morphine?"

He shook his head. He was not going to play this. He was too good as a cop.

"Ok, so assumedly it's the morphine in Georgie's room. It's...vanished?"

He didn't blink; he just lifted his mug and drank. No, not vanished, then.

"Ok, the medicine isn't Georgie's? Maybe a different name on the label?"

Thomas was perfectly carved from ice, setting his mug down again like he had all the time in the world.

"Give it up, darling," Pippa said, shaking her head and laughing softly. "He's good."

"I'm better. I have watched every episode of Crime Busters, including the unaired pilot." I said, leaning forward, squinting my gaze so I was focused entirely on Thomas, who was watching me with a bemused smile. "There isn't enough medicine gone to be a lethal dose?"

There!

A tiny, almost imperceptible twitch at the apple of his cheek. He still sat like a damn statue, but there had been movement. I grinned and slapped my hand on the table. "That's it, isn't it?"

"I don't know what you're talking about," he said, but his voice was ever so slightly strained.

I carried on as if he hadn't spoken. "So there's not enough gone to kill someone. Which begs the question, how did Georgie die of a morphine overdose?"

"There could have been a second bottle which the killer took with them. And left the other one to avoid suspicion," Thomas pointed out. "Not that any of this has happened, mind you."

"Of course not," I said, playing along.

"We checked Isaac's medical bag. A spare bottle, sealed. Georgie's medical records show he was issued two bottles the day before he died."

"So both bottles are accounted for?" I asked.

Thomas nodded. "You're starting to see why I have a headache?"

"I am. This is intriguing."

"Well, if you figure it out and find me a plausible suspect with motive, means and opportunity, then please give me a call."

"I still haven't got a phone."

"Buy a phone. Then give me a call."

I nodded bitterly. "I did buy a phone, but it got destroyed. Anyway, stupid question, but I don't suppose there's any way the autopsy could be wrong?"

"Always a possibility. I'll get it checked."

"Or maybe he just died. He had terminal cancer."

"Maybe. We may never find out the truth."

Thomas drained the last of his coffee and nodded his thanks to Pippa as he got up to leave.

"Are you staying over tonight?" I asked.

"I wasn't going to work late today. Until we catch The Jaw-breaker, there isn't anything urgent I need to do."

My face fell, and I nodded my understanding, not trusting myself to speak.

A tiny smile quirked the corner of his lips. "But if the invite stands even if I'm not here for work, then I'd be very grateful."

My blush returned full force, and I nodded so hard that the injury on my head flared up again. But I didn't care.

"Yes, please."

"See you tonight," he said.

Little love hearts were flying around my head and in my eyes as I sank back in my chair, grinning like an idiot.

Pippa sighed and whacked my arm. "Oi, lover girl. You forgot to tell him about the prison."

Oh right. Damn.

Seventeen

Luna says that our human and the detective like each other. And that they need time, space and perhaps a nudge.

Well, I can nudge. I can do subtle. I can do romantic.

Just watch.

--Thoughts from Loki

We closed the café just after six. Oli flipped the sign and locked up while I waved him and Pippa off and left in the opposite direction. It seemed I was healed enough that they trusted me to find my own way home. Small miracles.

When I returned, Thomas' black Mercedes was parked outside my house. He hadn't been kidding about finishing early; this was practically part-time work for him.

Once inside, the delicious smell of freshly cooked lasagne wafted through. So he'd been here a while. Wow, it really must have been a slow day on the case. Or he didn't want to deal with desperate solicitors staking claims on Georgie's estate.

"Hi honey, I'm home," I called, hanging my thin brown jacket on the peg by the door and kicking off my ankle boots.

"In the kitchen," Thomas called.

"I figured that dinner wasn't cooking itself," I said as I entered and leaned against the doorway, watching him bend to peek in the oven and offering me a fine glimpse of his derrière.

Thomas closed the oven door and waved a hand at a stack of letters on the kitchen table. "Post arrived."

"Yes, it has a habit of doing that each day," I said, bemused, as I picked up the pile and sifted through the few letters. Still so many subscriptions and things addressed to my aunt, even though she'd been dead a few months now. I'd have to do another round of cancelling catalogues and offers.

"It does. But post usually has the decency to wait on the doormat for the owner to get home."

I froze, my gaze unfocused on the Comfoot shoe catalogue in front of me. "I have no idea what you mean."

"I haven't touched the post. It was there on the kitchen table when I got in."

"Well, must have been there this morning. Wow, look, forty per cent off in this sale. I might have a look through it. I need some new slippers."

"Willow, there was no post this morning when we left. I was sitting right here," he tapped the back of one of the dining chairs. "There were no letters. We left for the pharmacy–"

"I came back," I said quickly. "After you left, I came back home and had to wait for Pippa to drive me to Norwich. The post came then."

Thomas' lips pressed together, the cogs whirring in his mind. I fought to keep cool, calm and not blush to the roots of my hair like I had a habit of doing when I was lying through my teeth. Luna would have brought the post in for me. It had to be her; Loki would have chewed a corner.

"What is this?" I asked, dropping the rest of the junk to the kitchen table and holding up a thick, creamy envelope.

"Willow, I just want to know–"

"No, seriously, this is from a solicitor. Oh god, maybe I've been speeding, and it's a fine?"

"It wouldn't come from a solicitor. It would come from the traffic department," Thomas said, edging closer to me. "Willow, this is serious. If someone broke in again–"

"What, and moved my post for me?" I asked, shaking my head and attempting a laugh. "No, I think...oh. Oh. Thomas, look, it's from those people that are harassing you."

I waved the letter under his nose and watched the tension gather in his shoulders. I felt bad about changing the subject away from my dead cats, but I knew this would distract him and make him forget about the post that seemingly had legs of its own.

"Yes, that's the one," he said through gritted teeth. And I mean properly gritted. His teeth were glued together, yet he still managed to speak clearly.

"Says they've been trying to contact me by telephone." I thought about my smashed mobile, sitting pitifully in my bed-side drawer. "So now they're writing. As the next of kin for

Dawn Addison, I'm being added to the joint claim for reclaiming historical losses from Georgie Weaver."

Thomas' brow creased as he idly picked at his hands, the blisters still looking raw but less red. "Your aunt lost money to Georgie Weaver?"

"Yes, I found something in her paperwork the other day. She lost about seven grand to him; he was doing her accounts when she ran a gardening business. She used to take me with her sometimes if I was staying around hers. She used to do a bit of weeding or landscaping, nothing too much. But I guess she needed an accountant to make sense of the tax and stuff."

"Are you going to pursue it?"

"No. Seven grand would be lovely, but it's not worth the fuss. I never knew it existed until a couple of weeks ago, and it was gone a long time ago. Can't miss what I never had, right?"

I smiled and lifted the sheet of paper, ready to rip it in half, when Thomas' hands covered mine, stopping me from destroying it.

"Are you doing this because you think it will cause me extra work?"

My lower lip caught in my teeth, and suddenly I had no idea how I was supposed to respond. He'd made it sound like such a big deal earlier, and I didn't want him to think I was money-grabbing.

He took the piece of paper and stared at it carefully as if it were evidence. "This was your aunt's money. It belongs in your family. Georgie Weaver stole the lives and dreams of too many people. It's only fair the money he inherited is repatriated to those he stole from. It can't bring back the dead; poor Frederick Wainwright will never know peace, but perhaps his family can. I'm told he has a daughter who has passed her medical studies. I imagine she racked up a fair amount of debt, and a payout would help her out right now."

"So, you're going to go to work tomorrow and sort out that paperwork?" I asked with a grin.

His lips curled into a faint smile. "Without complaint. I get it now. This is important. I just have to get the info for the freedom of information requests, the sooner I get that over to the solicitors it's out of my hair and onto their workload."

"It is. I hope that young woman gets her money."

We were leaning close now. I wasn't sure who had started drifting first, but it was like a magnetic attraction, with the two of us pressing close, mere inches from our lips brushing together.

Then the alarm blared.

"Dammit," Thomas said, spinning around and opening the oven door.

"No, wait!" I called.

Too late.

He grabbed the glass dish in his bare hands. Hands that were already injured from the stinging nettles. He swore again, and in slow motion, I saw the dish head for the ground. I could do nothing. I just watched it break clean in half as deep red sauce and melted cheese splattered all over the grey tiles of the floor.

We stood silent for a second, with the fire alarm wailing at us.

"Are you alright?" I awoke from my daze and hurried over, almost slipping on the sauce and cheese.

"Fine, just...ow."

"Come here. Put your hands under the cold tap."

I stood with him holding his wrists to stop him from withdrawing his hands too soon as cool water raced over his now doubly red raw skin. It was hard to tell what damage had been done over the top of the stinging nettle rash, but the pain receded fairly quickly, and it didn't look too bad.

He'd dropped the dish immediately, a saving grace from an injury perspective.

"I'm so sorry," he muttered. "This was supposed to be a lovely dinner; instead, there's nothing to eat, and I broke your dish. You're going to tell me it was a family heirloom or something, aren't you? One your aunt used every weekend when you stayed over?"

"I could say that, but it would be a lie. It was a fiver from Tesco."

"Oh, thank god, at least I don't have to worry about smashing your childhood memories."

"Sweet that you were worried about it, though. I'll buy another one next time I'm in town."

I sat on one of the dining chairs, inspecting his hands for open wounds, when he coughed discreetly.

"Hm?" I asked.

He nodded to the floor, where the fallen lasagne was cooling.

But he wasn't looking at the lasagne. Not really. He was looking at the smudged paw prints leading away from the mess. A cat caught red-pawed.

"Uh…" I said intelligently, stalling for time to enable my brain to devise an excuse.

"You said your cats were dead," Thomas said.

"They are."

"And I didn't see a cat in here just now."

"No, you wouldn't have."

"And yet, those are cat paws."

"They do look a bit like paws, don't they?" I said, making a show of squinting. "Funny how the sauce fell like that, isn't it?"

"They lead all the way to the hallway."

"Amazing how far the mess spread, isn't it?"

"Willow," Thomas said firmly. "What the hell is going on? That night when The Jawbreaker was here, I heard a cat screech, and then he looked as if something had attacked his leg."

"I think he stepped on a lego."

"What is going on?" Thomas asked, his hazel eyes looking straight into mine, searching for answers.

"You wouldn't believe me," I muttered, lowering my gaze.

He dipped his head, trying desperately to meet my eyes again. "Try me. Because right now, all I can think of is that, I don't know, your cats are zombies or something?"

"Ghosts."

"Sorry?"

"Not zombies, they're ghosts. They can turn solid at will."

"Ghosts. Ghost cats?" Thomas said slowly.

"I told you that you wouldn't believe me."

"I didn't say I didn't believe you. This is just a lot to take in." He glanced at the paw prints again as if reassuring himself that they were actual paws. "And the cats live with you here?"

"Yes. They come and go like regular cats. Go out hunting. Bring back things. Like live cats."

"Right. Ok."

"Remember Eleanor Catchpole's locket? The night of her murder, you came to ask if I'd heard anything, and you saw her locket on the floor behind me?"

"Oh yeah," Thomas said, snorting with laughter. "That was the reason you got dragged into the case."

"Exactly. That was Loki, one of my cats. He was out hunting, found it and brought it back because it was shiny."

"That's incredible."

"Unbelievable more like."

"No. But I need a little bit of time to process this."

"Take your time. Take all the time you need," I said, placing my hands gently on his injured ones. He didn't pull away, so he couldn't think I was that crazy. "While you're making up your mind, shall I order pizza?"

This time his smile was much brighter and he pulled his hand away just long enough to hand me his phone. "That would be great."

Eighteen

Loki has been telling me about his namesake, the Norse God of Mischief. It fits him perfectly. I can't believe he made himself known to the detective! But now it's all out in the open. I think it gave the poor man a bit of a shock.

Still, I've noticed that Willow has been calling him Thomas instead of Bardot. Things are moving forward.

--Thoughts from Luna

The following day when I shuffled downstairs in my dressing gown, Thomas was finishing up a conversation on his phone, deliciously wearing only a pair of navy boxers, matching navy socks and a grey t-shirt crumpled from sleep. His auburn hair stuck up and needed a good brush or for me to run my hands through it.

I yawned widely, tiredly waved a greeting in his general direction, and poured myself a coffee from the already-brewed pot.

The sweet, warm aroma was drifting up from my cup just as Thomas set his phone down on the table. "Maybe hold off filling those claim forms."

"Oh? A problem?" I asked, sipping the coffee, which was much too hot but contained the essential caffeine needed for life.

"Yes, a problem called Maria," he said, chuckling softly at his own joke.

"Too early for puns," I said, sipping my too-hot coffee. "Always too early for puns."

"Maria Weaver, to be exact."

I almost choked on my coffee. "Weaver as in *Weaver* Weaver?" I gasped.

"Yes. Weaver Weaver."

"But his wife died. It was in the news articles I read," I said, desperately performing a search function in my brain to bring up information on Georgie's personal life.

"Maria is his daughter. She turned her back on her father a long time ago. We've been unsuccessful in contacting her for days. And now she's come to us."

"Lucky," I said, then with the help of the few caffeine molecules I had ingested, the meaning of this new development caught up with me. I made a face. "She's going to claim his inheritance, isn't she?"

"I imagine that's why she has stepped forward," Thomas said. "The fact Georgie received a significant sum before his death was all over the news last night; someone leaked it early. I'm not surprised it got out with so many people part of this giant claim."

"So she came sniffing when there was money but didn't care enough to see her father before he died."

"To be fair, her father caused untold misery to dozens of families and drove a young father to suicide."

"You make a good point. Continue."

"She's insisting that I meet with her right away. I imagine she wants to get things sorted quickly before the claims can go through the system."

A long sigh escaped my lips as I glanced at the folded letter on the kitchen table. Seven grand. "Easy come, easy go."

"Exactly. It's a shame, but–" Thomas' phone buzzed with a message. He frowned at the screen and typed furiously. It buzzed again. His frown deepened.

"Something wrong?" I surmised.

"Campbell has told her I'll speak to her right away."

"That's ok, isn't it?" I said.

"As in right now. As in, he's told her I'm staying here and has given her directions."

"Here?" I echoed, my grip on the cup in my hand loosening. "*Here* here?"

"Yes, here here."

"Oh god, but the house is a mess, and I'm wearing my dressing gown, and this isn't exactly official, and how long have we got?"

Knock knock

"He spoke to her on the phone," Thomas said sheepishly. "She was already in town."

I glanced down at my fluffy slippers that had once been cream but were now dusty and brown. The fluff had matted into clumps. My bare ankles had not been shaved in over a week, and my dressing gown had holes in the hem where Loki liked to claw at it.

Thomas caught me appraising my outfit and huffed a sigh. "What about me? I'm the one doing the interview."

"I don't suppose if we hide behind the sofa, she'd think we weren't home?"

A tap at the kitchen window had both of us jumping and spinning around to find a heart-shaped, jovial face smiling at us. "Yoo hoo! Sorry to call so early, but can I come in and have a chat, please, detective? It's quite important."

I looked down at Thomas's clothing. He looked at mine. Our gazes slowly rose, and we mirrored each other's grimaces.

Five minutes later, Maria Weaver was sitting on one of my kitchen chairs, sipping coffee that had been brewed for me but that I had graciously donated to our guest. My only consolation was that I didn't have any guest mugs of my own, so I was dipping into Aunt Dawn's stock. Maria's beautiful peach gel nails were curled around the handle of a garish pink mug with a cartoon pig and the caption, "I didn't fart my arse blew you a kiss".

She looked less than impressed when I handed it to her, but it slightly evened up the fact that Thomas and I were in our nightwear.

"Detective Constable, let me start by thanking you for your work in this case. It's been a terrible ordeal, as you can imagine."

Thomas raised an eyebrow. From somewhere, he'd procured a notebook and pencil – ever efficient. "Interesting that you say that. We've been trying to contact you for nearly a week."

"Oh, well, you know. I changed my number fairly recently. You might have an old one."

"Of course," Thomas said, his voice silky smooth but with an undercurrent that Maria didn't pick up as her shoulders relaxed, thinking she had gotten away with her lie.

While Thomas ran over the investigation details to bring her up to speed, I took the opportunity to observe. Her accent placed her from Norfolk. She wore a busy floral print blouse over tailored cream trousers and a pair of high-heeled shoes with red soles on the feet tucked under her chair. She wore a single gold bracelet laden with charms on one wrist, and as I tried to stare into her eyes to check their colour discreetly, I simultaneously dredged my brain for what Georgie's eyes had looked like.

Hers were grey-blue. His had been an olive-brown mix.

Flags began waving in my mind, compelling me to complete my critical analysis. Georgie's skin was leathery from his years in the sun, although his tan had faded from his time in prison. Maria's was alabaster pale, smooth and silky. I couldn't imagine the lotions she used to keep it looking so good. She had to be in her fifties, but she looked decades younger.

The hair was a good colour match. The photos I'd seen of Georgie in the past had been black and white copies from newspaper print editions, but when I had seen him in person, his greyed hair had held a hint of the rust it had once been. His wiry beard was dark ginger. Maria's hair was a perfect deep orange match like the setting sun.

A light perfume wafted over from her...no, not perfume. Something else. I inhaled deeper and leaned slightly across the table.

"Are you alright?" Maria asked, staring at me as if I'd just smelled her hair.

Which, I realised, I nearly had done. I was much closer to her than I'd realised.

"Sorry was just...sorry. I like your perfume. What is it?"

"I'm not wearing perfume," she huffed, then turned back to Thomas, physically turning in her seat to present her back to me.

"So, as I was saying," Thomas said, shooting me a confused look. "You'll need a solicitor, and you'll need to go down to the station in North Walsham. The inheritance and claim itself is nothing to do with me."

"But you will put a stop to those other fraudulent claims, won't you, dear?" Maria asked, leaning across the table and taking Thomas' hands in her own. I wouldn't have touched them with a barge pole: they looked like he had chicken pox.

"I will speak to my team to ask for solicitor requests to be put on hold while your case is being verified."

"Fabulous! I knew I could count on you. So many people wanting what is rightfully mine. Don't they know the stress and stigma I have gone through my entire life? Living under the shadow of my criminal father. The money is my inheritance. Any claims were settled long ago with the sale of his house; surely they can't drag all this up again now?"

"As I said, that's for the law to decide."

"Well, thank you for your help," she said, standing to leave. Her coffee was still full. Clearly she hadn't cared for the mug. A petty part of me was glad to see that she had a smear of something orangey-brown on the shoulder of her blouse, hidden between the flowers. Even Maria couldn't be perfect.

"Oh!"

I was startled when she cried out, wondering if Loki had sunk his teeth into her ankle. I wouldn't have blamed him at all, but I would have thought he had better taste than this plastic woman who smelled of some strange, overly perfumed artificial smell.

"Those damn solicitors. Even you? Figures," she said, picking up my letter and ripping it in two.

My breath caught as I watched her let the two halves float to the table with a smirk.

"Good day to you."

Ugh, her smile was as fake as her hair colour.

Wait, hair colour? What was wrong with her hair? It was rusty bronze, almost red in the light. A very similar shade to her father. But something was wrong with it. It was solid. The colour had no variation at all. The reddish smear on her blouse.

She'd dyed her hair. Very recently. That explained the weird perfumed chemical smell.

Before I could say anything, she was gone. My hands balled into fists, nails digging into my palms until Thomas rested a hand over mine.

"We can always tape up the letter. It's fine."

"What a horrible woman!"

"I know. But then look at the genetic material she was working with."

"Doesn't excuse her being a bitch," I muttered, gathering the letter pieces and stuffing them back in the envelope for safekeeping. "Stupid horrible woman with her stupid perfect nails and stupid dyed hair."

We sat silently for a moment as if re-energising after the flurry of activity.

"Will she get to keep the money?"

"Probably. She's not wrong. It's probably too late for them to claim, and when Georgie was sentenced, his house was sold to raise some capital against the losses and legal fees. Mainly the legal fees; there was hardly anything left over from the repossessions."

"That's sad. I don't care about my aunt's money. Like you said a week ago I didn't even know she had lost it. But those people. The Wainwright family lost everything. Not just money."

Thomas nodded, his thumb running over my knuckles. His skin was still raw and red and calloused. "I know. Life isn't always fair."

"But think what that money would mean to the daughter Frederick Wainwright left behind. Money can never make up for a loss like that, but she would be able to pay off her medical school debts and live comfortably. More than comfortably. It just feels wrong to be this way around."

"Well, maybe Maria Weaver is needy too? It couldn't have been easy for her to have a criminal father. I imagine that followed her around like a spectre wherever she went."

"As if," I spluttered. "Her skin – she obviously has treatments. Her nails were expensive. Those shoes were designer. Her teeth and face have had work."

"That's not my business," Thomas said.

"No, but she doesn't need the money. Whoever Frederick Wainwright's daughter is actually needs it. Would rebuild her life with it."

"Like I said, life isn't fair. If the law says the money belongs to Maria, it belongs to Maria."

"The law? Or who can afford the most expensive solicitor?"

Thomas stared down at our joined hands. For the first time, his mask cracked as he found himself unable to defend the law. When he sighed, his shoulders slumped.

"No comment."

Nineteen

A century of experience has taught me that life is fleeting. My own passed relatively quickly, although of course I benefit from an afterlife on Earth. I'm not sure if humans can too, I've seen the ghost hunter television shows and it all looks fake. I don't think humans are smart enough to avoid the temptation of the bright light.

Luna refused to speak to me after I showed myself to the detective. Just a few paw prints and a little nuzzle.

Our human was taking so long explaining it that she'd die of old age. It cleared the air, the secret she'd been hiding was out in the open. Now things can progress for them.

See? I was helping.

--Thoughts from Loki

"Two words," Pippa said when I entered the café. "Cats. Where?"

My nose creased into a frown. "That's not a sentence."

"I didn't say it was a sentence. I said it was two words."

"I know, I know. I will keep looking. I will find us some suitable cats. I swear."

"Willow, I love you to pieces, but a cat café is false advertising if we don't have any actual cats. We pushed the opening day back once; we can't keep doing that. We need to book the local paper to come, and we need some influencers to be here. It needs a lot of arranging. To cancel again–"

"I will find a cat."

"Cats. Plural."

"I will find cats," I said, my anxiety creeping up a notch. Two cats was plural, right?

"I'm just getting a little anxious. Now that the media circus has packed up and gone home, trade has dipped again. We're living off Bardot's money, and I hate that. I want to get our business plan into operation."

"I know, I know. But I just need to do this one teeny weeny thing first."

Pippa's eyes narrowed at me.

"I promise it's small. I just need to do a bit of research, see if I can find Frederick Wainwright's daughter online." I sat on one of the tables and took out my tablet, trying to remember the café wi-fi password.

"Why?" Pippa asked.

I took a deep breath, then launched into a detailed account of my morning so far, including a) how embarrassing it was to do an interview in your lingerie, and b) how the woman looked like a porcelain doll. I finished it off with a sob story that Frederick

Wainwright's daughter was drowning in medical student debt and how unfair it was that someone like Maria would get all those millions.

When I paused for breath, Pippa jumped in. "I meant, why are you looking for her? She never left."

"She what?" I said, caught off guard. "She's here? Where?"

"Well, not here in the café," Pippa said, rolling her eyes and my naïvety. "She works at the pharmacy. She's a pharmacist. She got her degree at Cambridge and took a job here in Catton Strawless about a year ago."

"Oh." The wind was completely knocked out of my sails as I stared at my tablet. I hadn't even needed to connect it to the internet. "So, Chloe? *Chloe* is Frederick Wainwright's daughter?"

"Yes, you didn't know? I thought everyone knew everyone here."

"I'm still new here, and she doesn't have her surname on her name tag. I only know her as Chloe."

"Well, now you know. Poor girl is really bad at showing her emotions. I think her father's suicide really affected her, knowing that he chose death over being part of her life. But she's super bright; she got into Cambridge, after all. She's like a robot, I've been to the pharmacy a few times, and I swear she can diagnose and treat anything better than a doctor. And she's so young!"

"I guess she channelled her grief into studying. I suppose there are unhealthier coping mechanisms." I was thinking of the crowds of people gathered on the grass just to catch a glimpse of Georgie Weaver and yell their anguish or pelt him with fruit.

"Exactly. So maybe turn that tablet on and start looking for cats?" Pippa said with a pointed smile. "Or a phone. You need a damn phone."

"But I already bought one recently! Ugh, I hate this. Fine, but I want a different one. I didn't really like my new one; it didn't sit in my hand right like my *old* old one. I don't like them too big or too small. They have to be just right."

"Alright, Goldilocks. How about we head into the city this weekend for a shopping trip, and you can touch and feel them to your heart's content?"

"Sounds perfect, thank you. I don't deserve you."

"You really don't. Take my phone in case you get into any trouble or you need my advice."

"Thank you times a million."

"Yeah, yeah. Now find me some damn cats."

Damned cats would have been easier to find. Ghostly feline spirits are everywhere, and there's no risk of them being injured or stressed by the café patrons as they were already dead.

The downside to populating the café with ghost cats was pretty obvious – nobody would be able to see them.

My long-term plan did indeed feature ghostly felines, but to start with, we needed some cats that the customers could actually take pictures of.

I searched. I scrolled. Websites of local rescue centres as far as Suffolk. Cat and pet charity sites. Social media pages of local residents looking to sell their pets. On a folded napkin, I scribbled a few likely cats documented as being friendly, calm and could be housed with children or other pets. I added phone numbers and got to calling, arranging three appointments to meet a total of seven cats.

"Good work," Pippa said when I finally put down the phone (her phone) to the last shelter.

"Seven candidates. I'll go visit, talk to the staff at the shelter and see how the cats are. Sometimes they have a habit of saying friendly when actually they're shy. I don't want to bring any cat here that will be scared or stressed."

"No, I get it. But we want to give homes to as many cats as possible, right? Give them love and a home and all the cuddles they want."

"Exactly." I stretched my arms above my head, grimacing at the *pop* of my shoulders. I'd sat down for too long, but I had more sitting to do as I drove around the county looking at cats.

"Well, put a reserve on any you think would be a good fit, and then we can discuss them later."

"Yep, will do," I said, gathering my things. "See you later."

Ten minutes later, I had my satnav programmed and was zipping down the A140 to Drayton, just on the outskirts of Norwich. The weather was unseasonably warm, and I inched the window down to let the late summer air ruffle my hair.

The radio hummed throwback pop tunes that reminded me of my teenage years. And with getting to spend the day petting cats, I was in a pretty light-hearted mood. The thought of the injustice of Maria's inheritance and my own lost seven grand were firmly left in Catton Strawless, and with every mile I put between me and my problems, my body relaxed further.

The "House of Paws" was first on my list, and I nudged into one of the four parking spaces outside the single-floored square building. From the outside, it looked tiny, but once I was inside, I could see how far back it stretched.

"Can I help you?" asked a woman virtually bouncing on the balls of her feet. She wore a green polo shirt with the company logo, which clashed horribly with her bright ginger hair.

"I'm Willow Addison. I just called about the cats?"

"Oh yes, it was me you spoke to. I'm Hayley." She reached out a hand and shook mine, gripping it like she was playing tug of war.

"Hi, Hayley."

"So we had three cats you were interested in meeting?" she said. Her accent was thick Scottish, pleasant to the ear, but she spoke so fast it was hard to keep up with her.

"Yes, three cats."

"Adorable, they all are. Come round, my pet. We'll introduce you."

She led me through a door from reception into a maze of rooms. They were light and airy, with good ventilation so that they didn't smell of animal waste or wet fur. Always an occupational hazard in these places.

There were dozens and dozens of large cages lining each wall, each with bowls for food and water and some toys. But they were all empty. Instead, cats dotted the floor like miniature trip hazards, as if they were playing a game to test our dexterity.

As Hayley picked her way through them, none seemed inclined to get out of her way. They knew they were in charge, and they moved for no human. I followed Hayley, cautious not to step on any of the tails squiggling like snakes against the tiled floor. As I passed, one tom raised his hind leg in greeting and began licking himself.

"Here's Bagel," Hayley said.

I'd liked Bagel even before Hayley had mentioned a single thing about him on the phone. The name was so cute. And so perfect for a café. I really hoped he would be suitable for us.

Bagel was a brown tabby with a long fluffy tail that liked to curl back on itself to make a circle, like a bagel.

"He was a stray, not chipped, so we named him because his tail does that curl thing. Looks just like a bagel. Also, I'd had a bagel for breakfast the morning he came in, so maybe bagels were on my mind," Hayley explained.

"Bagel?" I called, sitting down on the tiles and crossing my legs.

A good start: Bagel didn't need telling twice. He sprang into my lap, paws scrambling against my jeans to find purchase. Then he turned around, making himself comfortable, walking from one leg to the other as he sniffed me, testing to see if he liked me.

"He's a sweetie," Hayley said. "Very cuddly. He's only been on the market a couple of days but has lots of interest already, so you'll need to be quick if you want him. He's so affectionate, but he does need lots of attention. You said you were running a café? With cats?"

"Yes, Oh!" Bagel butted my chin with his head, forcing my head up and rubbing his scent on me as he went. "I mean, the cats won't be serving or anything. That would be weird. Basically, cats wander free around the café, so customers can have a coffee and a cake and sit with them."

"I think it's adorable. And Bagel would be a great choice; he loves people. Can't get enough attention, can you buddy?" she scratched his head, and he leaned over to her, his hind paws still on my leg. He wanted to be on both of us at once.

"He'll be perfect. Can I reserve him?"

Hayley frowned, her fingers moving to under his chin. "Like I said, lots of interest. If you want to be sure of getting him, then I'm afraid we need to seal the deal now."

"As in pay now?"

"As in, take him now," Hayley said. "I have a litter of kittens coming in this afternoon and calls of a stray that somebody picked up and wants to hand over. I need the space."

I bit my lip, looking down into Bagel's gooey yellow eyes. He was back in my lap fully, as if he understood that he needed to ramp up the cute to force my hand and go against common sense.

Buy me. He was saying with his eyes. *Bring me home with you.* He conveyed with a flick of his whiskers.

I hesitated.

But not for long.

"I'll take him!"

Which might have been ok. I could cope with one live cat. But I ended up taking two more, too.

I cancelled the other appointments. Something told me that my weak-willed nature would have caved instantly, and I'd have been going home with seven mewling cat carriers instead of just the three.

How was I going to explain this to Pippa?

How was I going to look after them until we opened?

Oh, who was I kidding? My heart was full to burst. Three cats were getting a loving new home, where they would be fussed over to their hearts' content.

I was grinning like an idiot as I turned off the radio so I could listen to the new cats serenade me as I drove back to Catton Strawless.

Twenty

My human is being cagey. Something is up. She's doing something she shouldn't and something I wouldn't approve of. I just know its. I can feel it in my bones. Or at least I would if I had bones.

What is she up to now?

--Thoughts from Loki

The second I parked outside my house, the reality of the situation sunk in.

Three cats.

And two ghost cats.

We hadn't decided on who would home them yet, so I would have to settle all three newly rescued cats into my own home for now. Feed them, water them, change litter trays, cuddle them, love them, reassure them.

The worry lines on my forehead melted away. I couldn't wait.

The carry cages had been securely placed in my car boot, and I carried out the two ladies first. They mewled even though I tried to keep the swinging of their cages to a minimum. As there was no vomit in my boot, I assumed that none of the new cats suffered from motion sickness, which was good as I'd only just bought the car after a murderer wrecked my last one.

I placed them on the ground, unlocked the door and then set them inside before returning to collect Bagel. His furry face pressed against the mesh of his carrier so that he looked like he had squares shaved into his fur.

"Welcome to Casa de Addison."

Three mewing cats responded, but it was hard to tell whether they were expressing appreciation for their new home, hungry, sick of being in the carrier or needing to pee. Or all of the above.

"Bagel, you first." The clip to his carrier was slightly stiff, but I managed to spring the door.

Before I could open it wider, he nudged it with his nose so it swung on its hinges and edged his big fluffy body out. Instantly his head dipped to the carpet, which he began snuffling, pushing his face against the pile as he drank in the scents. Obviously, I had done a terrible job of vacuuming as within seconds he was chewing something that he had picked up. I would need to keep an eye on him and ensure there was nothing dangerous about.

"Ladies," I turned to the last cages, the clasps on these popping open quickly.

One burst out as if ejected, circling her carrier as if to inspect her ride, then she leapt on top, slipped off the side, landed on her paws and shook herself off before darting away into the kitchen, where I heard her claws skitter across the tiles.

"Bye, Boo," I called. She was a cream cat with a brown patch over one eye and the energy of a Duracell bunny. Her bio had promised a loving, energetic and playful kitty. They weren't wrong.

"Now, Sage. Where are you?" I'd lost the third. My heart skipped a beat as I worried I'd left the front door open and she'd bolted, but the door was closed. A few seconds later, I found Sage sat exactly where I'd left her, inside the carrier.

"Oh, sweetie, you can come out now. You don't have to stay in there."

The grey short haired kitty looked up at me with giant eyes ringed amber but with large black inky pools for pupils.

"Sage?" I asked, holding out my hand for her. She sniffed it cautiously, her whiskers ghosting my skin and tickling gently, before deciding that she preferred the shelter of her carrier.

"Ok, well, you stay there for now, but I'll be back later. There'll be food and water in the kitchen if you feel up to it."

I had no way of knowing if she understood me, but there wasn't much I could do. A tin of tuna was opened and dumped in a spare cat bowl which I placed on the ground alongside another filled with water. I would need extra supplies as I couldn't expect them to share forever.

"Litter!"

Oh no. Loki and Luna had no need for a litter tray, so I didn't have anything to hand. Thinking on my feet, I dug through the spare downstairs room where I had dumped most of my aunt's possessions that I hadn't thrown away immediately and found some decorating equipment I had bought in preparation for once I'd got things tidied. The paint roller tray was sacrificed, and I shredded some paper towels to put inside.

"There. Toilet. Got that?" I asked.

My audience was not particularly captivated. Bagel's head was already stuck into the food bowl. Boo was trying to climb up onto the kitchen table. And Sage was presumably still in her carrier.

"Please don't poo on my carpet," I pleaded.

In many ways, it was like being back in school. Knowing I had done something wrong, let someone down but trying to lie my way out of it. In my mind's eye, Pippa became my old maths teacher, who I was forever trying to convince that my cat ate my homework.

Apparently, cats don't do that.

Especially dead ones.

"How did it go?" Pippa asked, leaning over the counter. There wasn't a single person in the café.

"Found three perfect ones." Not a lie. Just not the whole story.

"Brilliant. How much will that be?"

"Two hundred quid donation per cat to cover fees, spaying, and stuff."

"Well within our budget."

Pippa tapped a finger against her cheek in thought. "Is three too many to start with, do you think? Maybe we should pick our favourite two?"

"No, no, three is fine. They're all from the same shelter and get on well. It would be cruel not to adopt all three of them together."

"Ok. Well, you know cats better than I do. So...pics?" she asked, her face lighting up.

"Pics," I agreed, pulling her phone from my pocket and bringing up the gallery.

With every photo that she scrolled past, her smile brightened. Her concerns at adopting three cats at once faded when she saw their melty eyes, cute little question mark tails and adorable jellybean paws.

Then her face fell.

"That's your carpet," she said.

Oh no. I'd taken the photos when I got home, but I hadn't even considered that Pippa would recognise my hallway carpet.

"Willow," Pippa said calmly. "Did you buy them?"

I am terrible at lying, so I kept silent.

"Willow." Now she really did sound like my old maths teacher. The firmness of her voice compelled me to spill all my secrets.

"They were so cute, and Bagel was super popular. He's only been there two days, but tonnes of people have been to see him, and someone else might have bought him, so I had to do it!" I said. But it all came out as one word, which left Pippa blinking as her brain processed and retrospectively added in the spaces and grammar.

"You were supposed to put a hold on them."

"Look at their little faces," I whined.

"Willow, you have zero self-control."

"I know." I hung my head. Yep, I definitely felt like I was failing maths class again.

"How are you going to look after three cats?"

"I'll figure it out." I neglected to add that the three adorable fluffy bundles of joy were probably defecating on my carpet right this very moment.

Pippa rubbed at her eyes and set her phone down on the counter. "Well, they're your problem until we open the cat café. Ok?"

"Ok," I mumbled.

She sneaked another glance at Boo's picture. "They are adorable, though."

I dared a grin. "Aren't they?"

The door opened, and the little bell rang to announce our customer.

"Oh, are you closed?" asked a polished Norfolk accent.

Ugh. Maria Weaver. Come to spend her squillions of inheritance money on latte and cream cakes.

"We're open," Pippa said with a sunny smile. "What can I get you?"

"Skinny mochaccino, no whip, a dash of cinnamon stirred in, half a pump of vanilla syrup and chocolate sprinkles. But not too many sprinkles, mind you."

"Right. I better write that down before I forget," Pippa said, her panicked gaze catching mine.

"I'll ring that up for you while Pippa starts on it," I offered, taking that pressure off.

Pippa shot me a grateful look as she went to work on the monstrous order while I carefully rang up what I could remember of it.

"That'll be four-ninety-five, please. Cash or card?" I asked, channelling my inner Pippa and smiling as politely as I could.

"Cash?" she sneered. "Does anyone these days still hold something so uncouth?"

I blinked. "So, card then?"

"Yes, card." She snapped. Then her gaze softened, and she laughed a short, loud laugh. "It's you! From this morning."

"It's me from this morning," I agreed, pushing the card reader towards her.

"Sorry I didn't recognise you at first. You look so different, fully clothed. And your hair is brushed," she said in a faux-friendly tone that all women know is meant to cut right to the bone.

The card reader was shoved toward her with more force than was strictly necessary, hoping that it might fly off and smack her in the face. It didn't.

She faked a smile that was almost as fake as her hair colour and reached her manicured hands into her purse for a card.

And I am ashamed to admit to the little thrill of pleasure when it refused to let her swipe it, and she had to insert and tap in a PIN number. I nearly snorted immaturely when she got it wrong the first time.

"Damn thing, how am I supposed to remember these?"

"Yes, remembering four digits can be challenging," I said, in the same fake compassionate tone she had just used on me.

Her beautiful face morphed into a scowl, but she got it right on the second attempt.

"Here you go, here's your–" Pippa usually repeated the customer's order to show that she had got it right. "Coffee."

"Thank you." Maria snapped it up, then fixed me with a glare before turning on her heel and clopping out in her ridiculous red-bottomed skyscraper shoes.

"I don't think we've won ourselves a repeat customer there," Pippa said, not looking in the least bit disappointed.

"Ah, forget her. She's not staying long, just long enough to get her filthy inheritance."

"Oh?"

"I told you earlier about that awful woman who showed up at my house and demanded to speak to Thomas in his boxer shorts, right? That's her."

Pippa frowned, staring into the shop as if she could still see her. "That was Maria Weaver?"

"In the flesh."

"Weird."

"Oh yes, she is most certainly weird. And rude. And a bit–"

"No, I mean, it's weird."

"What is?"

Pippa reached for the card reader. I hadn't noticed the slip of blue peeking out, where Maria had forgotten to remove her card in her anger.

"Weird that if she's Maria Weaver, then why does the name on her credit card say Elizabeth Phelps?"

Twenty-One

I don't often agree with Loki but today I agree with Loki. Who on Earth are these cats? And what are they doing in our house?

Has Willow abandoned us, preferring live cats that the detective can see? Will she forget about us and the love we can offer even in death?

Surely not? I thought Willow was better than that...

--Thoughts from Luna

"Elizabeth Phelps," I muttered to myself as I aimed the key at the lock, missed, and then tried again.

"Phelps," I repeated. The name didn't ring a bell. But I was sure it was important, and I was desperate to settle on the sofa and break out my tablet to do some research.

The moment I opened the door, however, any thoughts of computer time vanished completely.

To their credit, I couldn't see any "presents" on the carpet (although they could have toileted in another room). But the noise. Oh god, the mews. If the residents of Norwich some twenty miles away complained of the racket, then I wouldn't have been surprised. Never before had I been so grateful for the remote location of my house in an isolated village.

"What on earth is wrong?" I yelled over the cat wails, not expecting an answer as they were, of course, cats.

Sage was easy to find; she was still in her carrier and had curled up into a dozing ball. How she was sleeping through this goodness only knew, but I didn't disturb her.

"Bagel? Boo?" I called, making my way through the kitchen. "Loki? Luna?"

I felt like a teacher calling the class register.

And there it was. It felt like I had walked into a turf war dispute. Bagel and Boo were close to the door, and Loki and Luna were near the oven, defending their territory.

All four cat's backs were arched, their tails aiming high at the ceiling. Fur stood on end; Bagel was now so fluffy he appeared to be the size of two cats. The cats were howling and hissing at one another, not attacking, more a show of aggression and distrust.

"What is going on?" I yelled. They ignored me and continued their standoff.

With a sigh, I assessed the situation, trying to put myself in their shoes. Paws. Whatever.

Team Ghost was obviously aggrieved that there were new cats in their territory. This was their space; to make matters worse, I hadn't even told them new cats were coming. In fairness, I hadn't intended to bring new cats here, but I was already in Pippa's bad books for that. I didn't need grief from my cats too.

There might also be a tiny bit of jealousy that these cats were alive and could be petted by anyone and eat regular food. Maybe they were worried that I was replacing them?

Team Life was probably scared witless. I knew that live cats could see ghost cats, but they probably hadn't expected to see any here, living in my house. In the home that they had just been brought into and expected to be their own territory.

Traditionally ghost cats roamed free, not really sticking around anywhere too long. Without humans to domesticate them and care for them in their homes they just led a nomadic wandering life and, from what I had seen, rarely interacted with other cats. They were starved for love and affection.

Not like Loki and Luna. I never forgot how lucky I was to have them and to be privileged to give them a happy afterlife.

Whatever the case, the two sets of cats had aligned themselves as factions and were battling it out in traditional cat fashion by trying to yowl the loudest.

"Quiet!" I roared.

That was enough. The growling stopped. The hissing stopped. Four pairs of eyes turned to me, all lighting up when they recognised me.

Instantly the angry sounds melted to purrs. Fur flattened against their backs, tails lowered and swung happily, and they all moved to wind around my legs. Four cats trying to worm their way around your ankles is enough to trip anyone up, let me tell you. Fortunately, I was still standing in the doorway, so I braced myself against the frame.

"Hang on, careful!" I warned as soft fur brushed against my legs, the pressure increasing as they vied for my affection.

Bagel's floofy tail reached up almost to my waist as he found himself between my feet, narrowly missing out on stomping over Boo, who was darting to and fro in an excited tizzy. It wasn't entirely clear if she was trying to nuzzle me or had caught sight of her tail and was on the chase, but the two pursuits seemed compatible.

My ghost cats were a bit more restrained in their affection. Loki had been with me so long that he knew he had a place in my heart and didn't need to earn my love, but he still felt the need to reassure himself by rubbing his face against my shin, scenting me and reminding me that I was his. It was amusing to see Boo, on one of her trips around my feet, whack him in the head with her tail. Loki shook his pelt and looked aggrieved but confused about what had happened as she was gone in a blur as fast as she had arrived.

Luna mewled sweetly by my other leg, nuzzling her cheek against my shoe and licking my jeans. I wasn't quite sure why, but it was adorable nonetheless.

"Guys, look, I love you all. And I'm sorry I didn't explain the new living arrangements before I left."

As if they understood, all four cats paused and sat down, their eyes blinking up at me as if waiting for me to continue and explain myself.

"Loki, Luna, we have some house guests. We will be making them feel welcome, got that?"

Loki sneezed as if allergic to the very idea of welcoming the newcomers.

"Oh, don't give me that, Loki. You are *not* allergic to cats."

"Mrow," he answered, turning his head away to look at something else that wasn't me.

"I mean it. They're here because I invited them, so treat them as guests. As family. They've been at a shelter and are ready for a new life. They don't want to be hissed at across a kitchen. Got that? Loki?"

"Mrow."

"Good. Now Bagel, Boo, you are both very welcome here. I'm sorry if you've had a bit of a hostile reception, and I'm sorry I had to leave so suddenly. But I'm here now, and we're all going to spend a lovely evening together. Okay?" My tone left no room for challenge. Even Loki didn't have a wisecrack purr for me.

Just as things were starting to seem a little more settled and everyone would make an effort to be civil, the front door opened.

"Willow?" Thomas called. "You know there's a cat in your hallway?"

"Yes, that's Sage. Leave her in the carrier; she'll come out when she's ready."

"Right."

Whether it was a testament to just how weird his life was getting with me or tiredness at life in general, I was thankful that Thomas didn't feel the need to argue or ask more questions.

In fact, when he entered the kitchen and saw me standing in front of two cats who, for all intents and purposes, looked like they were sitting patiently and listening to me with rapt attention, he paused, blinked, and then carried on crossing the kitchen.

"Is there enough tuna?" he asked.

"Some. And salmon. I'm going to need to do a shop tomorrow to get proper cat food, but tonight they can have fish again."

Thomas nodded, rooted in the cupboards and found a tin of salmon to add to the remnants of the food bowl.

Bagel needed no encouragement and wandered over to plunge his muzzle into the fish. Unbeknownst to Thomas, Loki followed him, watching with narrowed green eyes as he observed the other cat with a distinct lack of personal space. Without the secret magic ingredient, Loki wouldn't be able to eat that fish. But he could smell it, and he could pine for it.

Quickly I glanced at the strange litter box I had set out for the cats earlier and could have sighed with relief when I saw that the shredded paper towel had been shuffled about and that the top layer was damp. At least they were house-trained as promised, and they recognised a litter tray no matter how strange it looked.

"So. The cats." I said, feeling that I owed Thomas a bit of explanation.

"Yes, I noticed them too."

"They're for the cat café. But I got them a bit early." I reran my explanation to Pippa but at half speed so that Thomas could understand the words. "So now they need a home."

Thomas nodded, watching as Boo skittered from side to side, eating a little from the bowl, then clambering over Bagel and swallowing a mouthful from the other side before doing a dizzying lap of the kitchen and fuelling herself with another bite.

"They're quite the characters," I said.

"I think the little one is stuck on fast forward."

"Yes, she is a bit energetic. Maybe that will wear off."

Thomas nodded his agreement and then began searching through the cupboards for a tiny salsa dip bowl that had belonged to my aunt. He scooped some salmon from under Bagel's reluctant nose and carried the little dish out to Sage so she could eat in peace.

My ovaries exploded at the cuteness.

"Thanks," I said as he returned.

He shrugged as if it was the most normal thing in the world.

"Well, looks like I should stay a few more nights to help you with the new recruits," he said.

"That would be helpful."

"What shall we have for dinner?"

"My turn to cook. Let me whip up a stew."

Bagel's ears pricked up.

I sighed. "Not for you."

Twenty-Two

A truce has been called. For the sake of Willow, who we all (except Loki) agree is marvellous.

Bagel isn't so bad. He sort of plods about a bit, doesn't move too far from his bowl and sleeps a lot. He does snore though, quite badly. Boo is the exact opposite and can't sit still. She's very young, from what I can gather. Although she doesn't stay put long enough to have a lengthy conversation.

Sage worries me. She still won't come out of her carrier and won't talk at all to cats living or dead. There's an aura around her, something I can sense. Almost as if she is neither living or dead.

--Thoughts from Luna

After a nice meal and a night settling the cats, I had completely forgotten that I had wanted to research Maria Weaver. Or Elizabeth Phelps. I fell into a deep, blissful sleep knowing that Thomas was in the next room and woke overheated and suffocating with four cats sprawled over me.

"Seriously?" I asked my cat blanket.

The series of purrs that greeted me was enough to give me a headache. As cute as they were, could they not at least time the purrs together, so they made a harmonious chorus instead of clashing against one another?

"Look, if you want food, you need to get off me."

They seemed to accept that logic, or else they knew I would get up now I was awake. While dressing, Bagel helpfully brought me a pair of socks (to go with the pair already in my hand). Boo zipped over with a bra (I was already wearing one), and Loki, not to be outdone, brought me a tampon.

"Thank you. All of you." I took the items and placed them next to me on the bed to tidy away later. "But I won't get done any faster. Go. Shoo."

Once dressed and downstairs, I paused in the hallway to peek into Sage's carrier and wished her a good morning. She blinked at me. The little bowl of salmon was eaten, and her water bowl was empty, so that was a good sign. I took them both to refill.

"Good morning," I said to Thomas, who was sitting at the kitchen table munching cereal and reading something on his phone. A second bowl sat across from him for me. Bagel was stretching his long body, and the rascal could nearly reach it. I grabbed him and put him back on the floor.

"Morning. Nice day, bit fresh," he said.

"I was lovely and warm this morning as I slowly suffocated under a pile of cats."

He snorted and looked up from the screen. "Two cats is not a pile."

My mouth opened to correct him, then snapped shut. He hadn't mentioned the idea of ghost cats again since our first conversation, and I didn't want to push. He needed time to adjust.

"Feels like more when one of them is Bagel," I poured coffee from the pot and then rummaged for more tuna. Last one. I opened it up and fed all of them, along with some Psy Treats for the ghosts.

"What's new?" I asked as I finally sat down for my breakfast.

"You saw me less than eight hours ago."

"I meant with the case. You're in work mode, I can tell. You have that little frowny crease between your eyes."

He frowned more, deepening said crease. "Nothing new. Maria is progressing with her claim for the inheritance. It doesn't alter anything regarding the murder; it's a civil matter that I wish no part of."

"Oh! Speaking of Maria. That reminds me. Guess who moseyed into the café yesterday?"

"Cristiano Ronaldo?"

I kicked him under the table. Lightly. But still. "Don't be an ass."

"Do you want me to guess? Because honestly, this could be a very long game."

"It's a rhetorical question. I was building up the excitement."

"Well then, it had better be someone really good. Now I'm expecting a head of state, at least a billionaire, possibly even a minor deity."

"You're impossible!" I groaned, but I couldn't help laughing. And I loved his little smile, melting away those frown lines.

It struck me how easily we fit together. Teased each other, were comfortable with each other. A cold hole opened up in my heart when I thought about what would happen when Thomas returned to his own home. I had never felt lonely living alone before, but now I had glimpsed a life with him, the thought of going back to living alone was frankly terrifying.

"Ok then, who- oh sorry, need to take this. It's Campbell."

Frustrated that I had been cut off, I munched cereal while Thomas answered the call.

"Oh. That's great news. Where was he?... Huh, that was unexpected. Well, good piece of police work there. Is he at the station in North Walsham?... Oh right. I probably won't make it before he leaves, so I'll go straight to Norwich. No problem. Speak soon."

"Interesting news?" I asked.

"Very. Someone has brought in The Jawbreaker." Thomas stood up and rinsed his bowl and mug.

"He's at North Walsham?"

"No. That's the strange thing. He was picked up in Thetford, so no idea how he got all the way down there. But he's being taken to Norwich. I can't reach Thetford in time, so I'll go straight to Norwich."

Already he was slipping into his navy jacket and grabbing his keys from the kitchen table.

"Will you be back tonight?" I asked.

He didn't miss a beat with his answer: "Absolutely."

The answer warmed me through as we said goodbye, and a little trail of butterflies fluttered around inside my stomach. Only as I heard his car roar to life did I remember that I hadn't finished my story about Maria in the café.

"God dammit."

Refreshing my coffee, I found my tablet and booted it up, intending to do some solid research. I'd just got myself into the best comfy position with my tablet balanced on my knees and my legs under me with a blanket tucked under to keep me nice and cosy.

Everything was perfect, and I opened a new browser page just as I heard something shatter.

"Bloody cats!" I yelled, chucking my tablet on the sofa and reluctantly kicking off my covers, almost getting my feet tangled up in my haste.

I stormed into the kitchen expecting to see four innocent pairs of eyes and a smashed mug but instead found the room cat-free.

A strange cool breeze drifted across the room, and it took me a moment to realise that there was a star-shaped hole in the window. On the floor was a dusting of glass shards glinting like diamonds, and among them, a brick with a folded square of paper tied with thin string.

Without thinking, I hurried across to the window and pressed myself against it, trying to see if anyone was there. There was nothing. My car was untouched. The space where Thomas' car had been just minutes ago was empty. Not a soul stirred, just the trees waving their leaves to me in greeting. Or warning.

Quickly I checked that both front and back doors were locked, then made my way over to the brick to untie the note. The strange binding seemed to be something like dental floss, which seemed a bit of an odd choice.

The note was written in carefully sized block capitals, possibly to disguise the handwriting. It was short and simple, to the point, and the paper itself gave nothing away with branding. And as I read and re-read the note, a chill ran down my spine.

The killer had been in my front garden.

STOP HER FROM CLAIMING THE INHERITANCE OR THE BODY COUNT WILL RISE

Twenty-Three

What have we let ourselves in for here? Minding my own business I was, just having my second breakfast, when suddenly the heavens were falling in.

Strange hard rain all around. Now, I'm long enough in the tooth to have seen hail before. But this weren't it.

I had to stop the young'un Boo from stepping all over it. She was fascinated by it, she was but I could see it was dangerous so I got us out of there on the double.

Our little lady came running in after we were gone so I knew something was up, I did.

Those two ghosties were shocked even, so hopefully this ain't a regular occurrence.

I hope she clears it away soon, I hadn't finished my breakfast.

*--***Thoughts from Bagel**

My hands were trembling badly as I sat on the cold tiles of my kitchen and stared at the note. I didn't know what to do; leave it where it was so that the police could evaluate the scene or clean it up so the cats didn't hurt themselves?

Thomas was the obvious choice for help, but as I scrambled to my feet, the realisation that I had no telephone sank me to the floor again. I felt useless and stupid; I should have ignored my bitterness at losing another phone and prioritised getting a new one. But everything had moved so fast recently I'd felt completely out of control of events.

"Well, it's not like the killer was inside. So the glass itself has no value as evidence."

At least, that was what I reasoned with myself. Because I needed to go out of the house to get help or even go to work, and leaving the cats alone with broken glass and a gaping hole in my window, didn't feel safe.

With the brush and dustpan from under the stairs, I swept up the worst of it, then used the vacuum to remove any fine shards that might cling to their fur, which could be licked off when grooming. I still wasn't satisfied, so I also gave the area a thorough wash.

At that time, Bagel poked his head around the door, and Boo tumbled into the kitchen but froze when she saw me. It occurred to me they had been in here when the brick smashed the window and were probably terrified.

"Oh, sweeties, I'm sorry."

I sat on the floor and opened my arms, which they were both quick to rush into. We had a group hug, and honestly, I think I benefitted as much, if not more than they did. Their warm, furry bodies in my lap were a huge comfort. The little rumble of their chests as they purred and the way Bagel licked my arm as if tasting me was adorable enough to distract me from the fear that was burning away like a flame.

With a deep, steadying breath, I let them go, calmer and better able to cope with the third invasion of my home in as many days.

"Just the window to patch now."

The only thing I could think to do was tape a sheet of cardboard over the hole. The cereal box was sacrificed, and one panel became my window bandage. An inappropriately cheerful bumble bee smiled at me.

Arming myself with a rolling pin (god only knew what I intended to do with it), I did a perimeter check of the building and poked the bushes with one end of the kitchen utensil. Clear.

"Ok, guys, it doesn't look like whoever did this hung around. They wanted to send a message, and they've done that. I haven't got a phone, so I need to head out and get help. Stay safe. Hide if anyone tries to get in."

They blinked at me. In fear? Confusion? Hunger?

"I'll be back. And with proper cat food. And litter trays." I added shopping to my list of chores. So much to do, so little time.

After a quick check on Sage, who batted a paw at my finger when I reached into her carrier and turned her back on me, I locked up the house and made my way into the village.

Instinct drove me to make a beeline for the café. Perhaps the thought of seeing my best friend's face and maybe getting a warm hug to calm my frayed nerves was the deciding factor that led my feet there. But the sinking feeling of disappointment descended on me as I got closer and saw the dark windows. Guilt poured into me like sand through an hourglass, piling up at the bottom as I remembered it was my turn to open up. So not only was there nobody there to offer a shoulder to cry on, but I was also letting the side down.

Heat built behind my eyes, and I had to take a few breaths to calm my nervous system, which was set to critical. My mouth fought to turn down at the corners, and tears prickled in my eyes.

Determined not to cry, I balled my hands into fists and dug my nails into my palms, the pain helping to ground and calm me.

"Ok, what next?" I asked myself.

I needed a phone.

"Ok, how?"

Borrow one.

The morning was in full swing, but there were only a couple of people I could see on the high street, and I didn't know either of them by name. I felt too self-conscious to walk up and ask to borrow their phone.

That left one of the shops. The charity shop next door was staffed by elderly volunteers who a) may not even own a phone or have it with them and b) would spend an hour explaining how hard it is to get to see a GP these days.

Next to that was a music shop. I didn't know the eccentric man who ran it very well other than he liked earl grey tea and a cheese scone every lunchtime.

In fact, the nearest shop that radiated warm, caring vibes was the pharmacy. Instantly the tension melted from my shoulders; the pharmacy felt safe. And that was what I needed right now. My feet carried me there without having to consciously think about it.

Chloe was leaning over the counter, clutching her phone and staring fixedly at the screen. She didn't even look up when I entered.

"Morning," I said, trying for a forced peppiness that I wasn't feeling.

"How can I help?" she said in a mechanical, distracted voice.

"Bit of a strange one, actually," I said with an embarrassed laugh. She didn't even glance up. Clearly she had seen plenty of strange things being a pharmacist. I could only imagine people removing shoes and putting their feet on the counter to show her an ingrown toenail. "I actually need to borrow a phone."

That got her attention. And her hands clasped the mobile in her hands a little tighter as if she was afraid I would snatch it from her and never give it back. Despite her youthful teenage looks, she was only a few years younger than me, yet I felt a generational divide between us as I saw how closely she guarded her most treasured possession.

"What for?" she asked suspiciously as if vetting to see whether I intended to use it for armed robbery.

"To make a phone call. My brand-new phone met an untimely end a few days ago, and this morning some lovely cretin decided to smash my kitchen window with a brick. So I need to report the damage to the police."

Her eyes widened, clearly impressed by the action. Catton Strawless was usually relatively quiet, so anything like this was prime gossip.

"*Your* kitchen window?" she asked, which was not the reaction I had anticipated. "I thought that police guy lived there?"

My cheeks warmed, and I shifted on my feet, not wanting to explain the delicate nature of my budding relationship to someone I didn't know that well. I was starting to regret my choice of help for a phone.

"He's staying with me while he works the Georgie Weaver case," I found myself explaining, though I wasn't sure what that had to do with me borrowing a phone. "Sorry, I know it's a bit of an odd ask, but could I possibly use your phone to call the police, please?"

"Sure." She handed it over to me, slightly dazed at my strange request.

"Thank you."

I took it from her, noticing that she had the social media account of the police already loaded on the screen. Why on earth had she been checking that? Whatever. I dialled 101 for the non-emergency police line and waited to be connected, my gaze drifting to a shelf piled high with various shapes and sizes of plasters.

Once the call was answered, I explained what had happened and was rewarded with an incident number and a vague suggestion that somebody might turn up at some unspecified time to talk to me. The woman on the phone seemed highly irritated at my lack of contactable number so that this could be done over the phone and made a big deal of how resource intensive it would be to get an officer out to the middle of nowhere.

Chloe sparked to life long enough to offer me a square of paper from a notepad on the counter and a pen compelling me to purchase Viagra. Slightly perturbed, I scribbled the incident number down anyway, not that I thought I'd need it.

"Thank you so much for your time," I said sarcastically, hanging up.

"Sounds like it went well," Chloe said, accepting her phone back and looking a lot more relaxed than she had when I first walked in. Perhaps because her phone was safely back in her possession. Seriously what did she think I was going to do with it?

"I guess minor criminal damage to private property isn't worthy of a blue light response. I get that, but since it was obviously connected to the Weaver case, they might have at least offered to pass it on."

"They didn't?" Chloe asked, her face crumpling to a frown.

"No. She sounded like I was wasting her time, to be honest. Just wanted to get me off the phone."

"Maybe you could call the police guy you're living with? He'd take it seriously, right?" she asked, this time actually offering me her phone.

"Thanks, but I don't know his number off by heart. All my contacts are in my phone, which took a nosedive onto the pavement."

Chloe frowned down at her phone as if willing a phone number to appear on the screen.

"It's fine. The person didn't hang around, so I don't think there's any immediate threat. I cleaned up the glass, so my cats aren't in danger. I just need to get someone to fix my window, but I'll work that out later. Right now, I need to get my backside to work and open up the café. I am super late."

"But you'll tell him tonight, right?" Chloe asked, her slim fingers wrapping around the phone and holding it close to her, like some kind of strange technological teddy bear.

"Uh, yeah. I'll get it sorted. Probably just a prank anyway, like the woman on the phone said."

"I wouldn't be so sure. It's worth taking seriously."

I smiled softly at her concern. "Seriously, I'll be fine. But thank you. And thanks for letting me use your phone."

"Any time," she said, watching me as I left.

Only once the door was closed behind me did I feel the heat of her gaze leave my back. I shivered, a strange sense of unease running through me. But I shook it off quickly and hurried back to the café, this time ready to open up.

Two hours late.

Damn, I'd missed the pre-work breakfast rush.

Twenty-Four

I rallied the troops. I have troops now, you know. Since the live cats are going to be here I might as well put them to work adding their perspectives to the task at hand.

Not that it helped much, I couldn't get Boo to sit and listen, Bagel nodded off and Sage didn't turn up to the briefing.

Luna sat attentively though.

We had a sniff around the brick and the string. Strange string, nothing like we'd ever seen before. Very thin, plastic-like. Twine, perhaps? Gardener's twine? Though it smelled slightly minty, a bit chemically.

More research required.

--Thoughts from Loki

With the uniform of the barista apron tied around my waist, I felt a little calmer. I switched on all the machines and felt even better as they hummed to life and blinked happily at me. Everything was as it should be.

First, I poured myself a cappuccino and helped myself to a pre-made shortbread biscuit, not bothering to warm it up. The sugar helped calm the trembling of my hands, and by the time I was wiping crumbs from my lips, I was ready to face the world.

So I flipped the sign.

And sat in silence for thirty minutes until the door burst open with a flourish.

"Isaac," I greeted, straightening up from where I'd bent over the counter and nearly fallen asleep. The sugar crash was kicking in. "How are you doing?"

"Terrible. Terrible! It's all going wrong," he moaned, wiping his nose against the back of a grotty sleeve.

"Oh, come on, sit down. It can't be that bad."

"It's worse!" he declared, slumping into a chair so that his limbs splayed everywhere like a daddy long legs.

"Can I get you a coffee? Something to eat, maybe?"

Honestly, he looked like he could use it. The cream sweater he wore was filthy, the jeans torn at the knees and not in a fashionable way. His hair was unbrushed, his chin unshaven, and his eyes bloodshot underneath his crooked glasses.

"Please. Please. But I...could I possibly put it on a tab? Please?"

Memories of his last visit flooded my mind, where he had used the excuse of a loyal customer to get a free drink. His shaggy, unkempt appearance tore at my heart, though and before I knew it, I was brewing him a flat white and baking him a fresh cheese and bacon muffin.

He sat with his head in his hands, fingers tugging at his sandy hair, while I prepared everything as quickly as possible.

When I finally set the order in front of him, he devoured it faster than Bagel could eat up a dish of salmon. He even went so far as to lick his fingers once he was done. I considered making him a second, but he looked a little brighter by this point, and I wondered if he was up to talking.

"Isaac, what happened?" I asked, taking the seat opposite him as he pushed the now empty plate aside and drew his coffee close to sip.

"Georgie Weaver died, and I lost my job. Not only that, he didn't pay me. He didn't even have a bank deposit set up like he promised. I didn't get a penny of what he owed me. And now I have nothing. No money, no job."

He gazed down miserably into his coffee as if the flat white might hold answers rather than just caffeine.

"That's terrible. I'm so sorry. He seems to make a habit of screwing people over," I said. To be fair, he had been jailed as one of the UK's biggest con artists, so what were people expecting? The man had hardly been a saint. "Why didn't you have a contract?"

"It was kind of an unofficial gig," Isaac mumbled.

"What do you mean?"

Isaac shrugged and closed up. Literally and figuratively, he wrapped his long arms around himself and curled up in his seat before finally speaking. "Doesn't matter anymore."

"Well, what will you do now?" I pressed.

"I have no idea." His face brightened, and his eyes lifted to meet mine. "Do you need any help here? I can make coffee. I've never used fancy machines, but I could learn. And I can cook some stuff so I can help prepare food. Or take orders, maybe?"

My face twisted into what I knew was a pained version of a sympathetic smile. Even if we were hiring, I wasn't sure Isaac was what we were looking for.

"Isaac, you're still so young. Only just qualified, I guess? Why don't you try one of the NHS trusts? I'm sure they're hiring. Could you work in the community or a hospital? Even a GP surgery, maybe?"

His body deflated again like I had popped him with a pin. "You don't want me."

"I didn't say that. The café is only just surviving. Pippa was going to close down a month ago. But we're rebranding. It's a busy time, but finances are tight. We have an investor and are trying to be as frugal as possible. I'm sorry, Isaac, but we can't afford another staff member. I really think you should consider a nursing position, they're always hiring, and it's a stable job while you get back on your feet–"

The slam of Isaac's palms hitting the table rattled the plate.

"There is no getting back on my feet, don't you get it? I'm through! Finished! I have nothing. Less than nothing as I have a hotel bill that I'm somehow supposed to find the money for. He didn't even pay for my room like he said he would! I'm homeless and in debt, and no one will hire me."

"Isaac, why do you think no one will hire you?" I asked, reaching out to touch his arm, but he jerked back, almost tipping his chair over.

"You wouldn't understand! Nobody understands."

Now he was acting like a teenager during their years of misunderstood angst. But for a grown man to be throwing a tantrum, as young as he was, he was still an adult. It seemed a little odd. Then again, he barely looked out of his teens despite graduating from medical school. I was struck by his resemblance to Chloe, another bright medical student who looked so much younger than her years.

"Ok, Isaac. Explain it to me."

But he was too far gone now. He was on his feet, hands wringing in front of him, eyes darting everywhere. Tears rolled down his cheeks, and his breathing came out in shuddering puffs as if he were hyperventilating. Which he was, I realised.

"Calm down, Isaac. Sit down. I'll make you a cup of tea. Maybe the caffeine wasn't the best idea; I shouldn't have given you coffee. Or I'll get you a hot chocolate, maybe? Something soothing?"

"I can't pay!" He cried.

"It's fine, it's fine," I rose to my feet slowly, my hands in front of me as I approached him like a startled horse. "It's free. On the house. You don't have to pay."

"I can't pay. I can never pay. How will I go on? I can't go on." The words hit him like a revelation, his eyes widening, his face draining of colour. "This is it for me."

"Isaac, you're not thinking clearly. Sit down, please."

I reached out again, but he drew away sharply, almost comically tripping over his feet as he staggered away from my touch.

His long legs were like stilts, and he barely seemed to remember how to walk.

"Isaac?" I asked.

"I have to go. I can't...I can't anymore."

"Can't what?" I yelled after him.

But the door the café had closed behind him.

"Can't what?" I whispered to no one, an icy fist gripping my heart and squeezing tightly.

Twenty-Five

When I saw the poor lad run past, I was out and about just having a wander. Gathering my thoughts about who could have broken our window.

The distress rose in waves off him, he was certainly in pain. My heart reached out to him and I followed, keeping a distance but so that I could offer comfort if needed.

Although how I could do so I didn't know.

Fortunately, my human was on the case.

--Thoughts from Luna

It took me only a minute to grab my keys and lock up the café, but by that time, Isaac had vanished from sight. Part of me wanted to call the police, but rationally I had no idea what, if anything, Isaac was planning.

And I still didn't have a phone.

Something made me enter the pharmacy and rush up to the counter where Chloe was once again on her phone, eyes glued to the screen.

"Customer, Chloe," called a deep voice from the back room. Charlie, the owner, must be in.

"Help you?" she drawled, not looking up.

"Chloe, I need your phone again. Isaac, the nurse that was looking after Georgie Weaver, I think he's going to do something stupid. If I find him, I might need to call the police." Or an ambulance.

Chloe's eyes flew wide open. To her credit, she seemed to grasp the seriousness of the situation and appeared ready to help. Too willing as she literally jumped over the counter.

"Which way did he go?" she asked, already striding to the door.

"Wait, you're coming too?"

"Obviously."

"What about your job?"

"Oh yeah." She raised her voice: "Just going out. I'll be back soon."

Charlie's disembodied voice yelled something back, asking her where she thought she was going, but she had already slipped out of the door, so his words fell on deaf ears. I followed, not wanting to be left in the firing line if Charlie came charging out after us.

"Which way?" Chloe asked again.

"He just ran out of the café and then right. I saw him through the window; he went right."

Chloe said nothing but darted off, jogging down the high street and leaving me to putter along behind her trying to keep up. It didn't help that she was wearing trainers, and I was wearing a pair of pretty but uncomfortable pumps.

"What happened?" Chloe suddenly asked.

I was a good few metres behind her and starting to get out of breath, so this wasn't exactly the conversation I wanted to be having. But since she was taking the time to help, I supposed I owed her an explanation.

"He's been a little off for a while. But he came into the café saying that Georgie hadn't paid him, so he had no money. Honestly, I'm not exactly surprised. Georgie *was* a crook."

Chloe said nothing to indicate that she had either heard or understood, so I continued.

"Then he started getting upset and saying strange things about how he'd never get another job. He wanted to work in the café, he asked me for a job. Then he seemed to think his life was over and that he couldn't go on. Those were his words: that he couldn't go on."

"Idiot," Chloe muttered.

"Excuse me?" I asked, startled and defensive.

"Not you. Him. Come on. I think I know where he is."

"You do?" I asked, surprised again.

I'd thought I'd been asking Chloe to borrow a phone, but it looked like I had missed a stronger connection between the two. I suspected Isaac had a crush on her but was that perhaps reciprocated? Was she genuinely concerned for him? Was that why she had literally leapt into action to help? And why she knew where he would be?

All I could do was follow her, my feet rubbing painfully against the heels of my shoes and shaving off a few layers of skin as we ran.

"Where are we going?" I yelled between gasps for air.

Chloe didn't answer. I was sure she could hear me.

We had turned off the high street, down a few side roads, past the church, then down a cobblestone road that was lovely any other day, but running on it was like trying to make your way across a sea of oversized ball bearings. With every step, my ankle turned as my feet fought for a grip on the smooth round stones.

Chloe opened more space between us and then disappeared into the park.

Dashing to keep up, I almost sighed with relief as my feet met soft, springy grass. So much nicer to run on and less chance of breaking my ankle. Chloe wasn't too far ahead now; she was heading toward the lake and the little bridge that crossed from one side to the other.

A figure was standing alone at the apex, hands on the low wall, staring down into the dark depths.

Isaac!

Somehow my body found a burst of energy, and I sprinted the last hundred metres to where Chloe had stepped onto the bridge. I could hear her calling to him; her voice pitched low and soft as if she were coaxing a cat down from a tree. A cat that at any moment might claw her face off in fright.

"Isaac? Come on, buddy, what are you doing up here?" she asked.

He shook his head violently as if trying to shake off her words.

"I know it feels hopeless, but you'll be fine. I'll make sure you're fine."

"*How* Chloe?" he finally burst out, his voice hoarse from crying. "How can things ever be fine again?"

"I can make them right. I've got a lot of money coming. A lot. I promise to share it with you. You don't have to worry anymore. I'll look after you."

"Don't. Just don't, Chloe. Where would you get money from? Did you buy a lottery ticket?"

"Better. That arsehole ex-employer of yours got a juicy inheritance before he popped his clogs. Millions for the taking. His dumb daughter is trying to claim the inheritance, but I've got a lawyer working to make sure that comes down to the victims. I'm owed the six-hundred and fifty grand my dad lost, plus interest. Plus damages. Emotional and physical. I can wipe him out myself, and everyone will say, 'poor Chloe deserves it; she lost so much more than anyone else', and they'd be right. But I'll share the money. I'm not greedy. I don't need it all."

That was the most I'd ever heard Chloe say. It was probably her monthly quota of words because she immediately sat on the low wall of the bridge as if needing a break.

To my amazement, Isaac sat next to her, their shoulders brushing. I felt a bit voyeuristic, but they both knew I was there and hadn't told me to leave, so technically, I was kind of part of this moment too.

"Why would you? You could pay off your debts and go live in the Bahamas or something," Isaac said, a rustle of fabric as he swiped his filthy sleeve under his nose again.

"Because I promised, dork," she said, elbowing him in the ribs.

"Yeah, but that was just talk."

"Wasn't to me. I promise I'll look after you. As soon as I get that money, you and me, we'll leave this dump and go to the Bahamas together. Then it won't matter."

Oooh, what won't matter? I wondered, unconsciously leaning closer.

"You mean it?" Isaac asked in a trembling voice.

"Course."

Perhaps they hugged. Perhaps they kissed. I had no idea, but our attention was caught by a dog off its lead chasing after a tennis ball. It ran straight for the lake, and before I could yell or do anything to stop it, it galloped straight into the water with a loud splash.

Then bounded across, fording the lake easily.

Isaac looked down at the water, his reflection rippling back at him.

"Oh," he said. "I can't even kill myself right."

We walked Isaac back, one of us on either side of him, still not convinced he might not run away to find another puddle.

"You can stay with me tonight," Chloe offered.

Isaac's pale cheeks flushed, and he nodded without saying anything. Surely a first for him.

"Sorry. I know I was eavesdropping," I said, not sorry at all. "But what doesn't matter? When you're both loved up on a private beach, what won't matter anymore?"

"Oh, that?" Chloe said as if I'd asked her about the weather. "Well, it's Isaac's gossip."

His shoulders slumped, and I was suddenly worried for his mental health again. I was about to tell him to drop it when he spoke.

"Suppose it doesn't matter now. But...I don't have a nursing qualification. I never passed."

The sun was high in the sky and cast Isaac in an almost mythical glow of gold. As if by revealing his big, pent-up secret, he was somehow redeemed.

"You're not a nurse?" I spluttered. "Did Georgie know?"

"Oh yes," Isaac laughed darkly. "He knew. I was the only one that would take the job as his private nurse; all the qualified nurses said no. So we had a deal, he'd give me a job and...and forge a qualification for me. And I worked every hour at his beck and call for peanuts. Still, I needed those peanuts. I may not have qualified, but I still have the joy of all the debts from university."

"Wow," I said, which was the most pathetic thing I could have responded with. "That's quite a story. That's why you were so upset."

"My parents don't know," Isaac continued as if I hadn't spoken. "I pretended I didn't want to go to graduation, and I photoshopped a fake certificate for them to see. Georgie was going to get a friend to do me a proper forgery, but he never did.

And I'm glad. That was haunting me. But my parents would have been so disappointed to know I failed. I was screwed either way."

His voice lowered again, dipping back into depression. Chloe's promise – whether she could keep it or not – was a plaster on a gaping wound. Isaac needed help. A lot of help. And a lot of healing. I hoped, with or without the money, that Chloe could help him with that.

True to form, she slipped an arm around his waist and rested her dark blue-haired head on his shoulder.

"I went to uni with him. Met him in freshers year. He was doing nursing, and I was doing pharm, so we had a lot of classes together. We promised each other we'd both make it. But you can make it in other ways, Isaac. Your life isn't over."

He heaved a sigh, still looking upset.

We reached the pharmacy. I rested a hand on Isaac's free shoulder. This time he didn't pull away.

"I wish you the best. Both of you. Take care of each other."

Chloe nodded and led Isaac into the pharmacy.

The impromptu confession session had left me exhausted. I needed coffee.

And to open the café before we went bankrupt.

Twenty-Six

We all have secrets, I suppose. Loki more than most.

My secret isn't all that special; I took one of Eleanor's scarves before they started moving her things out of Woodburton Hall. I keep it under the sofa and sometimes I'll take it out and lay on it if I'm feeling sad. It used to smell of Eleanor but the scent is fading now. One day it will just smell of silk.

I wonder if Sage has a secret? Or maybe she would enjoy a turn laying on the scarf? It might comfort her. She's like that lad Isaac, deeply unhappy about something.

--Thoughts from Luna

"I need a new phone."

"Hello to you, too," Pippa said as she closed the café door behind her and began shrugging out of her jacket.

Before she had a chance to settle, I launched into an abridged version of events since we'd last met, as if we'd been parted for years, not hours.

Pippa ooh-ed and ahh-ed at the right points as I ran through the brick smashing through my window to Isaac's strange visit and subsequent flight. Then how Chloe had strangely insisted on joining me before a reunion that revealed he had never been a nurse at all, and Georgie Weaver had shafted him too.

"Jeez, how long was I gone?" Pippa asked, fake checking her watch.

"I know, right? And I *still* haven't had a chance to research Maria Weaver or Elizabeth Phelps."

"Darling sounds like you need to get your priorities in order. The police can sort out Maria; you need to get your window fixed. And tell Bardot about all of this. And get yourself a phone and maybe a rottweiler to patrol your perimeter."

A nervous laugh escaped my lips, and my legs went to jelly. Perhaps it was being with an old friend, someone who I knew would look after me. But the whole thing caught up with me. Being held at knifepoint. My home vandalised. Isaac's distress. I hadn't realised that I was being held together with blu-tac and was starting to come undone.

"Sit down. Breathe." Pippa gently guided me to a chair and kept her hands on my shoulders while I breathed in and out a few times, deep breaths that cleared my head and calmed my frazzled nerves.

"Where is Bardot?" Pippa asked.

"Norwich. They caught The Jawbreaker and took him in for questioning."

"Well, Norwich is a good place to be if you're looking for a new phone. Why not take yourself off and kill two birds with one stone? Tell Bardot what happened with the window and go shopping."

"But we need to work on preparations for the new opening," I protested.

"I will feel a million times better if I know you have a phone on you. I love you to bits, but you have a habit of getting yourself into awful danger. Do this for me? We can sort out everything else another time."

Hanging my head, I sighed. To be fair, I wasn't much help here now, anyway. My brain was not in a creative mode. I was stressed, tired, and desperate to speak to Thomas.

"Ok, I'll go."

"Fab. They still have that cute continental market on I think, can you pick up some of those Belgian orange chocolates?"

I grinned. "For you? Absolutely."

Spoiler alert: I forgot the chocolates.

My drive into Norwich was careful. My head injury still twinged now and then, but mainly, it was my nerves. I felt like I might jump out of my skin at the slightest provocation. I stuck to the speed limit, much to the annoyance of drivers behind me. At the nearest opportunity, they screeched past to overtake me with a lingering stench of burned rubber.

For the privilege of parking nowhere near where I needed to be, I had to pay £4.50. The card reader was out of order, and the machine was personally offended by the few pound coins tucked in the corners of my purse.

Finally, the fee paid, I hurried into town.

Phone first to give Thomas as much time as possible to be done questioning his suspect.

I dipped into the store that I had my contract with, explained what had happened, showed them my poor battered (yet otherwise brand new) phone and within half an hour, left with my second new handset of the month.

Next, I made my way to the police station on Bethel Street. I found myself hurrying, wanting to get there as quickly as possible. If I was honest with myself, I wanted Thomas' reassurance that this was just a prank. Maybe they'd had a spate of such crimes, and he would tell me it was nothing to worry about.

The station's double doors were propped open despite a light chill in the air. The floor was a black and white chequered pattern that made me want to move like a chess piece to get to the front desk.

A lady with greying hair scraped into a bun looked up at me behind a scratched Perspex screen. I wondered if it was bulletproof. Then I wondered why I was wondering about that.

"Hi, I'm here to see Detective Constable Thomas Bardot."

"Yup. Name, please?"

"Willow Addison."

A few taps of her computer later, her gaze was back on me. "Is he expecting you?"

"Probably not, no. Maybe I should have called ahead, but my phone is brand new, and I'm not used to it yet, and I'm rambling. You don't care about my new phone. Sorry, look, I just wanted a quick word with him. Please?"

"I'm afraid–"

"I'm his wife." What on earth made me blurt that out?

The receptionist looked as shocked as I did. "Uh, ok."

"I have something very urgent I need to discuss with my husband, but my phone is out of order. It's very urgent."

"Very urgent?" she repeated, still a bit taken aback by my aggressive claim to be married.

"Yes, um, I'm pregnant. And I need to tell him right now."

She lifted an eyebrow. "Right now? While he's at work? Could you not wait until he gets home? That'd be nicer right? You'll still be pregnant tonight. It doesn't seem that long to wait."

God, what was it with me and receptionists this week? Maybe they all hated me. Perhaps there was a league of receptionists against Willow. Or maybe I was just absolutely terrible at lying.

Oh well, in for a penny in for a pound.

"The baby is dying." Oh god, what was I saying? But the words wouldn't stop. "I'm now going to the hospital, and they're going to perform emergency surgery to save the baby. But there's a ninety per cent chance it could kill the baby or me. Or us both. I need to see Thomas before I go through with it, to say goodbye and let him know that I tried to bring his child into this world."

"So." She looked remarkably unmoved by my story. "There's a ten per cent chance you'll be fine, though?"

My palm slapped the Perspex screen. "Have you no humanity? This may be his last chance to tell me he loves me!"

For a long moment, she said nothing. Then she reached for her phone and dialled an internal number without ever breaking eye contact with me.

"Yup, it's me. Got Bardot's wife down here a bit hysterical."

We stared at each other while the line went quiet. Perhaps they were going to find Thomas. There was a faint voice on the other end, and then the receptionist put the phone down after thanking them, once again sure of her actions but not looking at what she was doing.

She was staring at me. And now she was smirking.

"Bardot says he doesn't have a wife."

"When I say wife, I mean fiancée."

"Didn't like your ring?" she asked, pointing her sharp gaze at my bare ring finger.

"Oh damn you!" God, even the receptionists here were bloody Sherlock Holmes reincarnated. No, he was fictional, wasn't he?

The door behind me clicked open. "Hello, wife."

"Thomas! You came!" I said, resisting the urge to stick my tongue out at the receptionist.

"Wife?" Thomas asked.

"I panicked. I didn't know what to say."

"Your name? Willow, you don't have to lie. I'd have come speak to you if you needed me."

A blush rose on my cheeks, and I was about to say something sweet and well-thought-out when the receptionist decided to land the finishing blow.

"Congrats on getting your wife knocked up, detective."

Thomas's hazel eyes fixed on me. My blush went from coy pink to mortified red.

"I told you I panicked. I may have bent the truth a little. We don't need to go into detail. Do we have anywhere private we can talk?" I lowered my voice. "And by private, I mean away from her?"

Thomas led me into an interrogation room and closed the door behind him. I glanced at the camera facing the small square silver table with a plastic chair on either side.

"This wasn't quite what I had in mind."

"Sorry, we don't have much space at the moment. No need to worry. It's soundproof, and the camera is off."

I nodded to the large mirror on the left-hand wall. "Do we have an audience?"

"No. I don't think so, anyway."

Taking a deep breath, I launched right in, conscious that Thomas was taking time out of his day for me. Even if he could have taken me somewhere a little nicer and perhaps even offered me a coffee or something.

"You didn't see who did it?" Thomas asked, sitting back in his chair and tapping his fingernails against the desk. His hands were healing nicely, although the skin of his palms was still salmon.

"No, they left pretty quickly. Didn't see a thing."

"Car tyre marks?"

"I'd have heard if they drove. I assume they were on foot."

"Footprints?"

"I didn't look. Maybe there's some by the window? But they probably threw it from the grass, so I doubt their prints would be in the flower bed. Can you get prints from grass?"

"Not often," Thomas admitted. "And you say the note was personal?"

"Here."

I dug the folded note from my pocket and spread it on the desk. He leaned forward to read it and kept staring at it for a long time as if analysing more than the words.

"Standard white notepad, although an interesting shape. Usually, they're rectangular, not square. Handwriting is disguised, so it's hard to tell if it's male or female. Generic ballpoint pen."

Part of me was damn impressed. "Have you done a course on this or something?"

"Only entry level. I'll have it analysed professionally, but there's a bit of a backlog and–"

"And it's not exactly a priority. That's fine. I just wanted to get your take on it. Do you think this is just a prank, or is it to do with the case? Is someone warning you? Are you safe? Are we safe at my house?"

His hand rested on mine, warm and solid and reassuring. His gaze never faltered as he sought out my eyes. "I promise you we're safe. We have Ricky Moreno as good as charged for the murder. No confession yet, but he'll break soon."

"That's good. I'm glad he's been found. But do you really think–"

"Who else?" Thomas asked. "He was there that night, argued with Weaver, and was owed money."

If those were the only criteria, then technically, Isaac was just as suspicious, I thought. It was even on the tip of my tongue to reveal what I had learned about Isaac, but I stopped. Snapped my mouth shut. What was the point? Isaac hadn't murdered Georgie because then he'd have lost his job for sure. So why bring it up? Why put him through an interrogation? He and Chloe deserved a second chance, with or without the inheritance money.

Although I wasn't going to land Isaac in trouble, I did want to raise my concerns about Maria. But just as I opened my mouth, the door opened.

"Sorry, didn't realise you were busy," said the man, pushing his glasses up his nose. "I'll come back."

"No, this isn't an interrogation. I just couldn't get a meeting room," Thomas said.

"Ok, well, in that case, the analysis is back on the morphine bottle for the Weaver case. That stuff is potent. It says two milligrams per millilitre, but this is way more. Way more."

"How much?" I asked, realising I was acting as if I were an officer.

"Twenty milligrams per millilitre." The lab tech said, flipping a page in the report he held.

A gasp escaped my lips, and I sat bolt upright as a memory flashed like a warning light. I had heard that number before. Recently. And it was important.

"Charlie," I muttered. "The pharmacist."

Thomas looked at me, a quizzical eyebrow raised.

"Remember? When we went in for the antihistamine. Charlie said morphine had gone missing."

The moment Thomas twigged what I was saying, I noticed the light flash in his eyes. "The bottle that went missing was this concentration."

"Exactly," I said. "So it really was stolen."

Thomas rose to his feet, scraping his chair back on the rough cement floor. "Or Isaac isn't as innocent as he's leading us to believe."

Yes. Or that.

Twenty-Seven

When my human takes herself off to the big city she should at least have the decency to take me with her. I miss the bustle of the city. In such an environment nobody notices things moving of their own accord. And there is so much to steal, so much trouble to make.

Very discourteous of my human not to take me.

Well, all I can say to her is good luck finding a matching pair of socks next week.

--Thoughts from Loki

"Faster, faster," I muttered, my knuckles turning white as I gripped the steering wheel. In reality, I wouldn't dare go a mile over the speed limit, but it felt good to tense my shoulders to the point of pain. It made me feel like I was doing something.

Right now, I was racing Thomas back to Catton Strawless. I had kept his black car in view for most of the trip, but at the last roundabout, a jerk in a BMW cut me off. I'd slammed my brakes so hard that my purse had fallen to the footwell and spilt its contents.

"Out of my way," I muttered to Mr BMW.

As if he heard me, the BMW sped up when there was a gap in oncoming traffic and zipped past Thomas, his exhaust spluttering and his engine roaring. I could imagine Thomas in his car, desperate to give chase as the guy was seriously speeding, but he was a detective on a mission, and he was on his way to make an arrest.

He hadn't said as much, but I could see that determined glint in his eye. The Jawbreaker didn't fit the crime. It was far too passive for a man that spoke with his fists. But the methods made far more sense when attributed to Isaac. I just couldn't place the motive, and it was bugging me. I thought Thomas was making a big mistake, but who was I to tell him how to do his job?

The sign for Catton Strawless gleamed in the early evening sun. I passed it quickly and breathed a sigh of relief to get a space at the market car park next to Thomas. His car flashed to lock, and I saw him striding off toward the pharmacy through my rear windscreen.

Why the hell had I told him where to find Isaac? I felt like Judas. Poor Isaac had bared his soul to me.

And if Thomas found out that Isaac wasn't a registered nurse, then he would count that as a motive, assuming Isaac killed Georgie to keep his secret safe. Fumbling with the seatbelt, I freed myself and ran after him, still wearing my non-athletic pumps, and waved my key fob in the vague direction to my car to lock it.

"Wait! Wait!" I called. Thomas had just slipped into the pharmacy, and I wasn't too far behind.

By the time I made it, I was out of breath, and the backs of my ankles were rubbed raw by my shoes again.

Nobody noticed my entry; they were already embroiled in a staring content. Chloe stood to her full height behind the counter, her dark gaze locked with Thomas'. Isaac sat on a stool and, because of his tall gangliness, was almost the same height sitting down as Chloe was standing up. He looked miserable; his head hung, his chin rested on his chest, and his back was arched over.

"I need to speak to Mr Green. Alone." Thomas' voice was calm but firm.

"Not a chance. You think I don't know what you're going to do? You're going to take him to prison for something he didn't do."

"With all due respect determining whether Mr Green has committed an offence or not is not your remit."

"You're just so bad at your job you're clutching at straws trying to pin this on someone, and you think Isaac is an easy target." She turned to Isaac. "No offence."

Isaac waved a hand but didn't look up. It was difficult to tell whether the wave meant he had heard and forgiven her for the mild insult or that he agreed with it.

"This is an active investigation, and I have to follow up on all leads. New evidence has come to light–"

"What evidence?" Chloe crossed her arms, perhaps trying to make herself look bigger. The blue hair didn't help; it made her look like a bratty teenager.

"That's what I was hoping to discuss with Mr Green."

Part of me wanted to intervene. Thomas was a great detective, but he was very formal. Very by the book. Chloe was so anti-establishment that his proper manner was probably only making things worse.

"Tough, Mr Police Officer Man. You want to talk to Isaac; you have to talk to me too."

"If Mr Green would like you to be present and if you were to assure me that you would not interrupt, we could arrange for a recorded meeting at North Walsham station–"

"Nope. Here or not at all," she said, shaking her head.

"But this is a public–"

"Here. Or not at all. Ten seconds to decide."

"Look, I don't want to escalate this, but you are currently in breach of the law, obstructing enquiries into an active murder investigation."

"Oh yeah? Well, what about our rights? Doesn't Isaac get a lawyer or something?"

"If Mr Green would like to instruct a solicitor to be present–"

"Whoa whoa whoa," I said, coming between them literally and figuratively. I stood between Thomas and the counter, holding up my hands, palms facing each of them. "This is just getting messy."

Chloe exploded. "What do you expect? He came barging in here–"

"Let's put that behind us. The detective just has a few questions about something that showed up on a lab report, a few things that we need to understand a bit better. Isaac is the best person to answer these, the only person really, and then we can go from there. Isaac can help us understand what we're seeing."

Chloe's scowl faded a little. She still didn't look happy, but then I doubted her face was capable of showing a positive emotion.

"So, just talking?" she asked.

"Just talking," I confirmed.

"No recording?" she asked.

"No recording," I confirmed.

Thomas touched a hand to my shoulder. "Actually we do need to record–"

I spun to face him. "No recording."

With that agreed, Chloe locked the door to the pharmacy, and we made ourselves as comfortable as possible on two little step stools used for stocking shelves. Chloe and Isaac retained the full-sized stools, and the counter remained between them and us.

"Can you tell me about Georgie Weaver's medication regime?" Thomas asked.

Isaac shifted on his stool, still looking down at his lap. "Don't you have a copy of his medical records?"

"Yes, but I'd like to hear his routine from you."

Isaac let out a long, low breath and blinked rapidly as if loading a file of information into his brain. Then he offloaded that data onto us with astounding accuracy. "He was on blood thinners, Clopidogrel in the morning and aspirin before bed. And lansoprazole in the morning for gastroprotection."

Thomas scribbled in his little notebook and nodded as if he knew precisely what Isaac was saying.

"He took a daily Atorvastatin tablet. Laxido for...constipation. And sometimes an antiemetic if he was feeling sick. Oh! And, of course, the morphine. But you knew that one. Obviously."

Thomas' hand quivered slightly at the final drug as if trying to keep the excitement from his posture and remain neutral. "Tell me about the morphine. I don't suppose you remember the strength?"

"Of course, he bloody doesn't! He was only that prick's nurse for a few weeks. You think he's going to remember the dose of every–"

"Two five milligrams tablets twice a day and a shot of another ten milligrams per five millilitres in liquid form for breakthrough pain, maximum of three of those in a twenty-four hour period."

"Right," Thomas said, scribbling it down and leaving us all shuffling in silence while he did. I had no idea why, as Thomas already had all this information. "That strength is fairly typical?"

Isaac shrugged a bony shoulder, finally looking up at Thomas now that he was on firm ground. For someone that had failed their nursing exams, the guy was knowledgeable. "Yeah, pretty typical for palliative."

Thomas tapped his pencil against the notepad. "How was Georgie to work for?"

Isaac huffed. "I told you before he was a nightmare. Always yelling and demanding I do things right away."

"And did you? Do things right away?–"

"Yeah, he was my boss. It was what I was paid for."

"So you'd do what he asked?"

"Well yeah."

The trap was coming. I could feel it like I was hurtling down a hill in a car with no brakes. I felt like Isaac's confidence was increasing a bit too much, a bit too early. He would need to slam on those brakes, and he'd soon find out they weren't working.

"So what would you have done if Georgie had asked you for more morphine? If his pain was so bad that he wanted another dose? Maybe a fourth injection of liquid morphine in one twenty-four-hour period? What would you have done then?"

Isaac's face drained of colour. He had tried the brakes and found them faulty. "I...uh...well, I'd have said no."

"You just said you'd do whatever he asked of you."

"Oh, come on–" Chloe said, but Thomas held up a hand to silence her.

"I suppose I'd...I wouldn't have...but he..."

"He asked you for more, didn't he?" Thomas pressed.

"Just a little. Not enough to kill him. Just a little, one or two doses shouldn't have been, I mean, with the other tablets and...he was palliative, it seemed unfair to...but he wouldn't..."

Isaac was not only crashing, he was falling off a damn cliff. Watching him physically twist in his seat was painful as he desperately tried to find a way out of the web he had woven around himself. Even Chloe looked pained, wanting desperately to defend him but unsure how.

"Isaac," Thomas said, loud and clear. "Did you give Georgie Weaver more morphine than his prescribed dose?"

"He told me to! He said he'd...oh god..."

"He said what?" Thomas asked.

Isaac shook his head, his lips turning pale as he pressed them tightly together as if desperately forcing the words to stay in his mouth. I was sure I knew what he wanted to say: Georgie had told him to give him extra pain relief. Otherwise, he'd fire him and reveal he was practising nursing without a qualification.

"You gave him extra?" Chloe asked, looking pretty pale-faced herself. I wondered if she appreciated the gravity of this. When it was found out – and it would be found out – that Isaac was practising illegally. Even she wouldn't be able to help him then.

"Isaac Green. Georgie Weaver died of a morphine overdose. I have no reason to believe that anybody else administered the drug to him. And you've now told me that you did indeed administer above the dose recommended by his doctor."

"Not that much!" Isaac cried, tears shining in his eyes. His voice cracked. "It can't have killed him; it was only a few more injections. It can't have done!"

Chloe was strangely silent, staring at Isaac as if she didn't even know him anymore. I supposed friendship and loyalty could only stretch so far.

"As you know, the liquid morphine used on the night of Georgie's death was of a higher strength than he was prescribed. And with the additional doses, this proved to be a fatal concentration."

"What? No. No, what?" Isaac spluttered.

"Isaac, I'm very sorry, but I need to take you in for further questioning. And this time, it will be recorded. And now you really may wish to consult with a solicitor."

"Oh yeah?" Isaac asked, his voice high-pitched and hysterical. "With what money? Should I sell my damn shoes? Would that help? I have nothing, man, nothing. In fact, I have less than nothing! Why would I kill him? I didn't switch the dose. I have no idea what you're talking about."

Thomas stood from his stool, standing tall and strong. "Will you please come with me?"

"This can't be happening," Isaac whispered as he stumbled around the counter and was led out of the pharmacy by Thomas.

"What will happen to him?" Chloe asked me in a quiet voice.

"He'll be questioned. He'll be kept in a holding cell. They're not as bad as you think. He'll be offered food and drink and be made comfortable."

Honestly, I had no idea if any of that was true, but it sounded like she needed to hear it right now. She had been so ready to defend him, but hearing the facts had broken her.

"Will you be ok?" I asked.

She didn't answer, so I took out my new phone.

"Hey, put my number in your phone. If you need anything, give me a call. Yeah?"

She blinked, registered what I'd said, then moved over to the rack of pegs on the wall. A single dark hooded jacket hung there, and she took her phone from the pocket and tapped in the number I gave her.

"He'll be ok," I said.

Her gaze rose to meet mine. "Will he?"

I couldn't answer that, so I turned to leave. As my hand pushed the door open, she called out softly.

"He didn't do it."

I smiled at her faith, but I couldn't share it. Now more than ever, I felt that we had the right person. But I felt terrible. In part, I imagined that Isaac had done it for her, to avenge her father's death.

Young love. Young lives wasted.

Twenty-Eight

Sage is tolerating my presence now. Not in the way that Loki tolerates presence, because that's just how he is. Sage yearns for contact but is denying herself it.

I sit outside her carrier and just talk to her, almost like a mother would. Or what I imagine a mother would say. I don't remember mine. Strange as I had never thought of myself as old and I'd never had a litter of my own but it came naturally. All the soothing words, all the ways to get her to relax and trust.

Eventually she said just one perplexing word: onion.

Perhaps she likes to eat onions? Even Bagel thinks that's weird and I've seen him eat a month old Cheeto from under the fridge. Maybe I misheard her.

--Thoughts from Luna

Thomas stayed over on Friday night. He returned late, in the early hours of Saturday morning, and then packed up his things and left for his own home in the morning. The case was all but closed; Isaac was officially being charged with murder.

The Jawbreaker was no longer under suspicion for the murder, but he had been kept in for threatening behaviour, public drunkenness and taking a hostage in her own home. I could still feel the edge of his knife against my throat when I closed my eyes and the hot breath against my neck as he pulled me close.

Saturday afternoon felt lonely and cold and empty.

Pippa and Oli ran the café while I prepped press releases and social media posts. We were due to go live on Monday, and we'd already started getting acceptances from influencers and local journalists who could promote us.

The only thing that kept me going was the cats. Bagel and Boo loved chasing one another around the house. Boo, an energetic little firecracker, and Bagel, more lazy in his efforts, taking frequent breaks.

Loki seemed put out by their outgoing nature and would often watch darkly from a corner, his back arching if Boo got too close or accidentally ran through him. He liked being in his non-solid spirit form around her as Boo skidded on the kitchen tiles and barrelled into him while he was munching PsyTreats. Since then, he had been very wary of her.

Luna sat sentinel at the mouth of Sage's carrier. She barely mewed or moved; she just sat there as a motherly presence. Once or twice I had seen Sage start to edge toward the opening to be closer to Luna.

I hadn't realised how much I'd enjoyed having Thomas at home until he wasn't there. At night I jolted awake whenever the wind rattled my windows, or a cat leapt with a thud, or a door creaked. So used to having him here, I felt vulnerable and terrified.

What if the person who threw the brick came back? What if the person got angry enough to do something stupid, like set the house on fire? Did they even know that Thomas wasn't here anymore?

As I drifted off, I realised I still hadn't researched Maria. Her fake hair dye, her fake name, everything was wrong. Was she really who she said she was? Or was she just a con artist like her father using a stolen or fake card? Or was it possible this was something more sinister and she was a true con artist who had slipped up by revealing her real name?

All the possibilities swirled in my mind, and I fell into a restless sleep where I stood alone in a greenhouse, and one by one, the windows exploded and rained glass around me, shredding my skin with a thousand painful sharp cuts.

I woke on Sunday morning to a sound I hadn't heard in a while; my phone ringing.

The ringtone was strange as I hadn't taken the opportunity to change to a new sound. Sleepily I patted my bedside table and finally managed to locate the phone.

"Hello?" I yawned.

"Good morning, sleepy head."

My lips curled into a drowsy smile. "Hey. Sleep well?"

Thomas paused momentarily, and I held my breath, praying that he would say no. That it was the worst night's sleep of his life, and he wanted to come and live with me forever.

"Not so bad. My neighbours had a party until the early hours, but I have some decent earplugs. You?"

"Oh yeah, fine," I said, deciding against recounting my greenhouse dream. "What's up?"

"I needed to pick some things up from The Windmill Inn. We're officially vacating the hotel. We're clearing Georgie and Isaac's rooms so they can be cleaned and reopened."

"That's good. I suppose now you have the killer behind bars, then you don't need to keep looking for evidence." It still felt wrong to associate Isaac with such a raw word as "killer".

Thomas sounded similarly uneasy. "Yes. Exactly. Well, it shouldn't take long, and I don't have anything planned for today. I recall you mentioning that The Mews and Beans Cat Café grand opening is tomorrow, and I wondered if you needed a hand with anything?"

My heart swelled so that I thought it might break out of my ribcage. Of course, I tried to play it cool and not sound too desperate. "Yeah, we could use an extra pair of hands. Lots to set up today and get ready."

"Good. Well, I'm free, is what I mean. And I'd love to help."

"One thing," I said, knowing I was being cheeky. "Can I come with you to see Georgie's room?"

I didn't tell him why. I needed to see the crime scene to assure myself that Isaac was the right person. That we hadn't made a dreadful mistake.

Perhaps Thomas was thinking the same thing because Mr Perfect Detective said: "Sure."

An hour later, I was showered, dressed and sitting in Thomas' black Mercedes as he edged into a space in the small hotel car park.

We bypassed reception and went straight to the first floor, where Thomas ran a key card over a reader, and the door clicked open.

Inside, the room wasn't as messy as I'd thought it would be. White bed linen was crumpled in a heap on the floor, along with a green woven comforter.

One of the pale magnolia walls had a dried stain where the bottle had smashed against it. Tiny shards of glass lay on the mocha-coloured carpet, the larger ones probably having been removed for prints. A little plastic numbered flag sat amongst them, indicating evidence.

Everything else was covered in fine fingerprint powder, but otherwise, it seemed in order. A paper pharmacy bag lay on a coffee table; probably all of the medicines had been taken for lab analysis.

A suitcase sat open on the floor underneath the large wall-mounted television. Inside, clothes lay rumpled, half folded, in no particular order. A pang of sadness reminded me that these were all of Georgie's worldly possessions.

My brain reminded me that Georgie had done this to himself. That he had owned many lovely things a couple of decades ago, bought with the money he had deprived others of.

Thomas picked up the set of evidence flags, a bottle of powder and a pack of gloves that had only been half-used.

"Ready?" he asked.

I blinked at his load. "You came back for those?"

"Yes, they're police property."

"Couldn't a tech or someone have picked them up?"

His cheeks coloured at the same time I realised that he had made an excuse to come back here. He had wanted to see me, and this had been the perfect way to do it. He said nothing but shifted his weight uncomfortably from foot to foot as if wishing for the ground to swallow him up.

"While we're here, can I see Isaac's room?" I asked quickly, trying to get over the awkwardness.

"Can't see why not."

Thomas led me down the hall, past a door, and swiped another key card.

This room was a mirror of Georgie's but was pretty much empty. Isaac continued using it until he was thrown out for non-payment, so his personal belongings were missing. Housekeeping hadn't cleaned this room either, though, and I could see that the forensics team had been over the room with their dust.

"Find anything in here?" I asked.

"No," Thomas said, sitting on the bed, staring at the blank television screen and clasping his hands together as he sank into deep thought.

I sat next to him, the mattress feather-soft under my backside. "Hear me out. If he did steal the stronger bottle of morphine from the pharmacy, surely he'd need to have tipped out the weaker morphine, probably down the sink and decanted the stronger one into Georgie's prescription bottle."

"Right."

"So what did he do with the bottle for the high-dose stuff? It wasn't in his rubbish bin or hidden under his mattress or anything?"

Thomas shook his head. "No, we turned the place upside down, searching for anything he might have left behind. But he used this room several days after the murder. And he could have done it a day or two before the murder. Housekeeping would have emptied his bin by then. It could be long gone."

I sank, literally, as the mattress was so soft. "Good point. But that implies he was planning it."

"Maybe he was? It turns out he doesn't have a nursing qualification. He was operating illegally. Georgie could have found out and threatened to expose him."

So Thomas knew Isaac's secret now. At least that was in the open, although when Isaac's parents found out on top of their son being charged with murder, I didn't want to think about Isaac's shame and what it might do to his already poor mental health.

The words tumbled out of my mouth before I could stop them. I supposed it didn't matter, as Thomas already knew. He might as well have the whole story.

"Isaac told me on Friday that he failed his nursing exams. He also said that Georgie hired him knowing that. Probably because he could get him cheap but also for the power he would wield over him. Whenever I saw Isaac, he was glued to his phone, jumping out of his skin when Georgie called him. If Georgie were in pain, he would have demanded that Isaac give him more morphine."

"Maybe so, but the concentration was still higher than the bottle stated, and it had been stolen. So Isaac had switched that out, knowing the higher dose would be fatal."

"Yeah," I said. It made sense. But it also didn't make sense.

But then, perhaps it wasn't supposed to make sense. I wasn't a murderer; I didn't know what drove people to do that. Isaac was a troubled soul, a complex character with fears, anxiety and a desperate need to please and be accepted.

And Georgie had been a horrible man, rotten to the core. Perhaps he had turned Isaac into a murderer? Had it taken much at all? The man had destroyed Chloe's life, and Isaac clearly adored her and would do anything for her. And Georgie had mistreated him as a nurse, with the constant threat of exposing his secret hanging over Isaac's head. Isaac was terrified of his parents finding out he had failed. Isaac had some serious mental health concerns. How much stress and anxiety could he take before he snapped?

How far are any of us from taking that leap to the dark side?

Thomas clapped his hands together in the traditional British way of announcing that it was time to go. "Shall we head over to the café?"

"Yeah," I said sadly, casting another glance around the room, willing something to jump out at me. A missing confession note hidden under the bed or something.

No such luck.

Not a shred of evidence to prove Isaac's innocence, and a whole mountain against him.

Twenty-Nine

Boo finally sat still long enough for one of my stories. Her paws were practically glued to the spot and her eyes were wide as saucers as I described her new home.

"Dogs. Dogs everywhere. Dog hair all over the floor. Pictures of dogs on the walls. And all there is to eat is dog food."

She almost, almost *believed me. Until Bagel ruined the fun and laughed his loud laugh and called out my lies. For some reason Boo chose to believe Bagel over me.*

Am I not trustworthy?

--Thoughts from Loki

"Left. Left. LEFT!"

"I think he heard you, Pippa," I called as Thomas and I made our way down the street to the café.

We had walked over from the Windmill Inn since it wasn't far, and Catton Strawless was an old-time market town built before cars, so it wasn't exactly overflowing with parking spaces. Especially one big enough for Thomas's large Mercedes.

"She lives!" Pippa turned to me, away from the men adjusting the new sign above the café.

The sign was amazing; cream background, "Mews and Beans Cat Café" in dark curly font with little paw prints on one side and the tall silhouette of an elegant cat on the other.

"Beautiful," I said as the men fixed the board into place above the door.

Pippa and Oli had scrubbed off the adhesive from the previous stickers on the large glass windows, and yesterday the floors had been varnished. All was going well ahead of the new grand opening.

"Sorry I'm late. There was something I needed to do," I said, hugging Pippa tightly. "But I brought an extra pair of hands, so that'll make up for what I missed, right?"

Pippa raised an eyebrow at me, clearly desperate to ask if Thomas had stayed the night. "Our benevolent benefactor is more than welcome but don't think it means you get out of some hard work, missy."

"Wouldn't dream of it." I rolled up the sleeves of my jacket. "Reporting in, ready to get my hands dirty."

Pippa's smile turned to a smirk. "Glad to hear it; you can start with the litter trays."

"Easy to assemble. That's exactly what it says: easy to assemble."

"I'm not saying it's not easy to assemble. I'm just considering the best approach."

Two hours later, Thomas was sat cross-legged on the freshly varnished wooden floor, trying to encourage a piece of wood into the slot of another piece of wood. They didn't quite look the right shapes, but that wasn't going to deter Thomas from trying.

Once more, I held up the little piece of paper. "Are you sure I can't interest you in the instructions?"

"There are barely twenty pieces. I don't need instructions."

"Kind of looks like you need instructions."

"It's not that I need instructions; the pieces aren't cut right. They don't quite fit. The machine that made them must have been on the blink. Do you still have the receipt? It may need to go back."

"Are you *sure* that's the right bit? Look, it doesn't quite look like the ladder rung. The end piece is the wrong shape."

"No, it's the right one. It just needs a bit of oomph to push it in. It's very tight. They need to cut these pieces better in the factory."

"I really don't think it's the right one. Why don't you try this piece?" I held out a similar piece of wood.

Thomas shook his head but accepted it anyway. "It's too short; it can't be the right...oh."

I waved the instructions in front of him. "Maybe try using the instructions?"

With a grumble, Thomas snatched them up and began to consult them. Three minutes later, the cat tree was assembled correctly with minimal fuss. And what do you know? Everything fit perfectly and had been cut correctly by the factory. I could barely hide my smile. For someone so by the book in his police work, Thomas was stubborn as hell when it came to DIY.

"What is taking you two so long?" Pippa asked.

"Now we know what we're doing, it'll be faster," I promised.

"There aren't any more trees. Maybe start unpacking the scratching posts? They probably come pre-assembled, looking at the size of the boxes."

Dutifully Thomas and I began on the scratching posts. One was a cute green cactus, another was like a giant pipe that the cats could squeeze through for fun, and some had strings attached with little balls to bat. They all looked great fun, and I wasn't even a feline. I had to bat the ball, and it hit Thomas in the butt.

"Sorry," I giggled.

"You're really not," Thomas answered, but he was smiling.

Food and water trays were set out, and tables were adorned with placemats and the new menus. A delivery came with ingredients ready for the next day, so we stocked the fridges and set out everything we would need for an early start.

Finally, we decorated for a party; balloons, streamers and a giant banner reading "Opening Meow!".

"We good?" I asked, resting back against the counter, which now had little paw prints painted on the floor leading up to it.

"Yeah. I'm nervous. Do you think this will be enough to turn our fortunes?" Pippa asked, leaning next to me and surveying our work.

"It will. People loved the café before, but they hated waiting. With the cats here to pet, people will want to stay longer. This is the perfect solution."

"Yeah, you're right. I'm just...nerves. I want this to work so badly."

"Me too," I reached for her hand and squeezed it gently.

"Ok, well, no more we can do. We're staying shut this afternoon, so I'm going to go home, have a really long bubble bath and try not to freak out," Pippa said with a nervous laugh.

"Take her home and help her relax, Oli," I said with a wink.

"Of course."

Her boyfriend wrapped an arm around her shoulders and led her out of the café, leaving me to lock up. Once we were outside, Thomas and I stood in silence for a moment, neither of us sure what to say.

"It's early–" I said at the same time as Thomas said, "So do we?"

"You first," we both said simultaneously, then burst into laughter. That broke the ice, and I felt much more relaxed.

"Want to come over and say hi to the cats? They could use some cuddles ready for their debut tomorrow."

"Sounds great. How is Sage? Has she made it out of the carrier yet?"

"A few times, I've caught her in the kitchen, but she always goes back. I think she likes the enclosed space. She feels safe, I guess?"

"Probably. Speaking of nervous people, should we check in at the pharmacy? See how Chloe is doing?"

"Good idea. I gave her my number in case she wanted to chat, but I guess she didn't want to chat." I frowned, glancing down the street at the pharmacy sign hanging from the wall. "It's good manners to see how she's doing, though."

In agreement and with a sense that we were doing our civic duty, we entered the pharmacy. Of course, Charlie was behind the counter, not Chloe.

"Welcome. What can I do for you?" he asked, scratching his broad chin. "Ah, Constable. Almost didn't recognise you in your civvies."

Thomas, who looked out of place without his uniform, shifted from foot to foot. "Yes, well, I was just wondering how Chloe was doing. Witnessing her friend's arrest couldn't have been easy. I wanted to check in with her."

Charlie pushed back his brown woollen jumper sleeve. The hem was frayed. It looked like a handmade jumper, thick and soft and slightly uneven. He glanced at his silver watch and then nodded to himself. "Well, she'll be here any minute; she's taking the afternoon shift. You're lucky. We only open every other Sunday these days. Not enough trade to keep us open, and with that new chain pharmacy just down the road, we can't afford all the hours we used to."

"A terrible state of affairs," Thomas said distractedly. "While I'm here, I was going to call in next week to tie off a few loose ends. We'll need copies of your controlled drug audit log book, staff rotas for the last three months and copies of personnel files and DRB checks."

"Goodness, all that?" Charlie asked, his ruddy cheeks flushing. "I would have to do a bit of digging–"

"Surely these are all standard files you should have easily to hand?"

"Well, yes, of course, but...you know how it is."

I was quite sure that Thomas did not know how it was and was silently judging the poor record-keeping. Honestly, I doubted if Charlie even knew what a DBS check was and suspected that a good word from someone's mother's nephew's friend's sister had been good enough to offer employment.

"Well, I can tell you that I haven't got to the bottom of it. I do have the logbook. It's handwritten, I'm afraid; I can't get on with computers. All it shows is that one week we had the morphine, and the next, we didn't. And now we have a new bottle in stock, and it's definitely one hundred per cent logged in the audit book."

"Staff rotas will confirm who was in over the period in question," Thomas pointed out.

"We all were. Well, at one point or another, anyway. We all do various shifts, but we've all been in since the audit was done."

Thomas' shoulders sank. "Well, I'd still appreciate copies. We may never be able to find who was on duty when the morphine was stolen, but I'd like to do my best. It's a loose thread, and I don't like loose threads. Any information you can give me might help. No detail is too small. Perhaps I can spot the moment the staff member was distracted, and someone could have gotten behind the counter to take it."

Charlie's bushy eyebrows met in the centre of his forehead like two caterpillars kissing as he frowned. "Well, that couldn't have happened."

"What do you mean?"

"The controlled drugs are in a locked box. The key is on the lanyard around our necks; see here." He turned over his lanyard holding his ID card, and a little silver key flashed in the artificial light.

"So there is no way a member of the public could slip around and take a controlled drug?"

"Unlikely. I suppose the box could have been left open, but I train all my pharmacists to open and lock it right back up straight away, not to leave it unattended. There's no reason to leave it open, and it doesn't get opened very often."

The creak of a door from the back room preceded heavy footsteps as Chloe stomped through. Her eyes were barely visible as the hood of her dark jacket was pulled up and slick with rain. Seeing us, her eyes opened wider, but she said nothing and took off her coat, revealing her flash of blue hair.

"So, like I said, I doubt it was a theft," Charlie continued, shrugging his massive round shoulders. "Beats me what happened to it."

"Well, copies of your stock ordering will help with that. We can trace the morphine through the system and pinpoint what happened. If you could please send me copies of orders and all transactions for the last three months, we'll start from there."

"Aye, that's a lot," Charlie scrubbed a large hand over his face. "Chloe, is that something you can do, please? You know how I am with the computers."

"Sure. If you tell me what you need and where to send it, I'll get everything you need this afternoon. It's always quiet on a Sunday, might as well get around to it."

She seemed too keen. Too willing to help, considering it was her friend she was incriminating. Perhaps she felt he deserved justice? Perhaps she, too, was doing her civic duty?

But as Thomas repeated what he needed, and Chloe wrote it all down, I noticed her notebook. It was perfectly square. Like the note that had been wrapped around the brick.

Thirty

Dogs? Dogs? I don't like dogs but I can run faster than dogs so I suppose it wouldn't matter if there were dogs at the café or not.

Loki lies a lot. I can see it in his eyes when he's lying, they get all big, or all small, or sometimes just medium-sized. Bagel says that you can tell when Loki lies because its every time that he opens his mouth.

I suppose Bagel could be lying but why would Bagel lie he seems very nice although he's quite slow and he can get in the way sometimes when I'm doing laps of the kitchen but I've learned I can jump over him if I time it just right. Sometimes I don't time it right.

--Thoughts from Boo

Thomas and I walked in silence down the road toward his car, and then, without even a covert military signal, we turned to one another at the same time and began speaking.

"I need to go to the station."

"I need to go home."

We both laughed a short, humourless laugh.

"I'm sorry. I wanted to have dinner together tonight, but I need to know how he did it. If Charlie says it couldn't have been stolen, how did Isaac get his hands on that high-strength morphine?"

"Chloe had a notepad similar to the note wrapped around the brick that smashed our window. Uh, I mean *my* window." A blush crept up from my neck to my forehead.

Thomas frowned, missing my slip-up and focusing on the safety element. "Be careful. Until I've tied everything up, I don't want you doing anything dangerous."

"What's dangerous? I'll go back to the pharmacy, ask for something out back and then grab her notebook so we can see if any of the pages have the imprint of the note on them."

Shaking his head, Thomas clamped his hands to his ears. "That is theft. I am not hearing this."

"I'll put it back!"

"And if you find anything, we can take it from there."

"No. I'm not putting that poor girl through anything else. She did it out of hurt because she thought she was getting one over on Georgie, taking back what he owed her family with interest. I understand why she wanted to send you a message if it was her. But I might try and guilt her into paying for a new window; those bloody things are expensive."

Thomas drew in a deep breath. "Just–"

"Be careful," I said, imitating his deep voice. I winked at him. "When am I not?"

"Now I'm even more worried."

We parted ways, and I went straight home. I did not pass go, and I did not collect two hundred pounds. I was a woman on a mission.

"Loki? Loki, get your furry butt here now."

No answer, but Sage peeked out of her carrier to investigate the noise.

Was there a sliver of onion shell beside her carrier?

"Sorry, my love, this isn't a job you can help with," I told her. As if she understood, she retreated to her safe space.

Loki was waiting out for an offering, I was sure. Heaving a sigh, I sprinkled a few PsyTreats into a bowl and set them on the floor. And waited. And waited. Little bugger probably knew I wanted something. If I hadn't, he'd have been here as soon as the treats hit the bowl.

Finally, after checking the time on my new phone several times and the anxiety within me growing to a fever pitch as the pharmacy's closing time crept closer, Loki poked his head through the wall.

"Hello to you, too," I said.

His whiskers twitched, and then he made his way over to munch on the treats.

"Those are down payment, Loki. I need you to do something for me. I know I always tell you not to steal stuff, but for once, I actually need you to do it, ok? I need you to steal a notebook. You know what a notebook is?"

"Mrow." Even cats can talk with their mouth full.

"A notebook is a book you write in. Look, it's like this," I grabbed a lined reporter notebook from my junk drawer in the kitchen and knelt next to him, showing him. He sniffed it, licked a corner, and realised it wasn't food.

"No, you don't eat it. You steal it. There's a woman who has one but square. You know square?"

"Mrow."

"Jesus, Loki, stop talking with your mouth full. Square is this." I put a hand over part of the notebook to remove the lower part and make it square.

"Mrow."

"Look, I don't care if you're not in the mood for burglary. I need you to do this. It's about protecting our home. I need to find out if Chloe broke our window because if it wasn't her, then I'm going to get a lot more freaked out as it means someone else out there wants to send us a strong message."

Loki finished his treats, sat back on his hind legs and began licking his front paws.

"Please, Loki? Come on; you got extra treats. And I'll make you more. I'll bake some fresh ones. Just for you."

He regarded me with his ghostly silver-green eyes. "Mrow."

Yes! The deal was struck.

"Come on then. We have to get going. The pharmacy doesn't open very late on Sundays."

How much Loki understood, I genuinely have no idea. He probably understood the words "steal" and "treats" and was on board. Whatever his motivation, he trotted along amicably by my feet as I grabbed my jacket again and left home. Just to be a brat, Loki waited for me to lock the door, then walked through it.

The sky was darkening, a molten gold sun dipping behind the buildings and painting pink steaks across the deep blue sky. Dark purple clouds scudded the skyline, thin but fluffy, catching the edge of the dying light.

In a hushed whisper, I ran through the plan again with Loki as we walked. "We both go in. I'll distract her while you grab the notebook and run home with it. Got it?"

Loki's tail swayed back and forth, so I took that as an agreement to my plan. It was probably the best response I was going to get. Honestly, I wished I could have taken Luna. She was much more reliable. But she would be mortified and probably morally object to stealing.

The lights from the pharmacy spilt out in the early evening dusk, the only shop still open at four on a Sunday apart from the garage. Catton Strawless didn't exactly have a buzzing nightlife scene. The best we could do was early-evening band-aids and haemorrhoid creams.

Taking a deep breath to steel myself, I rested a hand on the metal handle, facing the grimy glass of the pharmacy door and posters advising me of opening times and to book my flu jab (poster dated three years ago).

"Ready Loki?"

"Mrow."

My partner in crime sat alert at my feet, waiting for me to open the door despite not needing permission to enter. Even Loki's eyes were focused.

A chill in the air swept my blonde hair from my shoulders, and a shiver ran down my spine. I tried to push any ill feelings aside, but my instincts told me this was a bad idea. Thomas' voice echoed around my head, warning me not to get into danger.

But this was just a pharmacy. And it was just Chloe. The worst that could happen was we'd get into an argument about trespassing on private property and criminal damage to my window.

Right?

Thirty-One

What can I say? My human has good taste. When she knows a job needs doing right, who does she come to? Luna? Bagel? Boo? No, of course it's straight to Loki.

Although I had to put up a customary fight and feign nonchalance, truly I was energised by the mission. My favourite thing; stealing things! And I wouldn't get in trouble for it.

--Thoughts from Loki

"Hi again," I called cheerfully, hoping to draw Chloe's attention.

"Mmm," Chloe was on her phone, draped over the counter.

Seriously what was that supposed to mean? A greeting? An acknowledgement that I had been there earlier? Thanks for helping her stop her friend from attempting suicide? Anger that I had been there when that same friend was arrested for murder? I needed a bit more to work with.

"We didn't get to talk earlier, with the detective and everything. How are you doing?" I asked softly, sidling up to the counter to catch her attention. I glanced over the counter; her bag was dumped at her feet. I couldn't see a notebook peeking out of it.

"Alright."

Chloe must have reached her daily word limit. Or perhaps she was on a pay-as-you-go speech tariff. This was going to be difficult, especially as I couldn't see where the notebook was. I leaned closer against the counter, trying to see if it was on the desk with her. Her phone was logged on to a flight booking app.

"Have you heard from Isaac at all?" I asked.

"No. Doubt they'd let him call me, probably just his parents."

She had a point, but she didn't have to say it like I was an imbecile.

"Well, Detective Constable Bardot that he's being kept comfortable. Obviously in a cell, but it's not so bad. He's awaiting a hearing."

Finally, Chloe's gaze flickered up from the screen of her phone. "You spoke to the detective guy, right? Has Isaac confessed?"

"I don't know. But honestly, the evidence is pretty damning. Who else could it be? He was the one administering Georgie's medication, and his patient died of a morphine overdose. You have to admit it looks pretty bad."

Chloe chewed her lower lip. She was wearing dark mauve lipstick, almost purple. It went well with her hair, but as she dragged her teeth across her lip, little lines appeared, and the purple lipstick clumped at the tips of her front teeth. She didn't seem to notice, but I couldn't stop staring.

"He doesn't deserve any of this," she said sadly.

There! I spotted the notebook further down the counter, almost out of sight. It was perched on the edge with a pen on top, where Chloe had scribbled the words, "Amsterdam, 10-40".

Loki was behind the counter, so I pointed my gaze to the notebook until he finally got the hint and made for it.

"Does anyone deserve anything?" I realised I had to answer her, then realised that my answer was vague and meant nothing at all.

Chloe blinked, then nodded slowly. "That's really deep."

Was it? Well, whatever.

"Reminds me of university. I wanted to do literature, but my mum wanted me to be a doctor. I didn't get the grades, so pharmacist was a good second choice. But what I wanted to do was read and immerse myself in the stories of the past. The gothic era, the philosophical writings of the greats, you know?"

"Oh, cool. I had a friend in high school who was a goth," I said.

"*Gothics.*"

"Yup, them." Well, she was the one with dyed blue hair, a ring through the middle of her nose, dark eyeliner and a spiked bracelet. So sue me for assuming she liked the gothic or dark academia aesthetic.

Clatter

The pen fell to the floor when Loki grabbed the notebook. Panic rose with me, adrenaline dumping into my bloodstream as I lunged forward against the counter. "What was that?" I asked loudly.

"Just a pen. Loud pen," Chloe said.

"Yeah, they're heavier than you think," I said, faking my way through it as Loki padded around to my side of the counter, proudly carrying the notebook in his mouth.

"Weird, I thought I had my..." Chloe blinked and glanced around.

Distraction was needed before she realised her notebook was missing.

"By the way, you have lipstick on your teeth," I said, pointing to my own mouth as if she didn't know what teeth were.

"Oh, ew."

Chloe frowned and dug around in her bag for a compact mirror. She turned away from me for privacy and wiped away the lipstick. During those few moments, I crouched, grabbed the notebook and stuffed it into my bag. I was battling to get my bag zipped up again when Chloe turned back to face me.

"Well, if you're really doing ok, then I guess I'll make a move. It's getting late. You probably want to start closing up." Slowly I took a few steps backwards toward the door, not wanting to make any sudden movements.

"You know, now you're here, I have been having trouble sleeping. Maybe talking about Isaac would help?" she asked.

"Of course." Thrown by her desire to talk and now wanting nothing more than to leave and check her notebook, I reluctantly walked back to the counter and plastered on a friendly fake smile. "Anything in particular?"

"Just why he did it. I don't get it."

"No one does. Thomas is with him now, trying to understand more about the how. Your boss said earlier that he couldn't see how it could be stolen, so maybe Isaac was pulling the wool over all of our eyes."

"Maybe," Chloe said, her voice distant as if we were on different shores.

Abruptly she stood and walked over to a locked cabinet, which she opened with a key on a lanyard around her neck.

"See, the drugs are kept in here. We all have keys, and we always close it up again as soon as we're done."

The door beeped, and a mechanical lock clicked as the door sprang open. She reached inside and took out a small box which she held up for me to see.

"This is the same stuff that killed Georgie Weaver. Look, a tiny bottle. You wouldn't think this much of anything could kill a person."

When she opened the card packet and lifted the medicine, I had to agree; the little brown bottle was small.

"And it wasn't even all used. There was some left. So it's dangerous even if you don't give it all," I said, watching the liquid slosh about as she shook it.

"You know how it works, right?" Chloe asked. "It's injectable. Georgie was on regular tablets but then the injectable one for breakthrough pain. That's when even though you're on regular painkillers, you get pain anyway. The injection acts super quick as it's dumped right into your blood."

"I see," and this was all good information. I should have asked Chloe earlier to give me a background. Perhaps it would have led me to a revelation earlier that Isaac had been the one to kill Georgie.

And yet, I still couldn't make myself believe it.

"So how much would be lethal?" I asked. "Could Isaac have done it accidentally? Is there any way this is all just a big misunderstanding?"

"Let's see what volume the needle is," Chloe said, opening up a little plastic pouch within the box. "One millilitre. Honestly, Isaac would have had to inject a tonne of times to overdose at this strength. But then he would have had other needles. He was a nurse, after all. Let me see what we have."

She rummaged on the shelf behind her and came back with some more packets of individually wrapped needles.

"That's what I thought: the largest we do is five millilitres. With the morphine Georgie would have had in his system from the tablet and considering his general poor health, two of these would probably have been enough."

"Just two?" I asked, looking at the syringe she held. It was big but not *that* big really. So simple. Just inject and kill. Even someone like Isaac could do it. He wasn't the kind of person to kill with brute force, but by doing something he did every day, just at a higher dose, he could perhaps justify it to himself.

But why? My mind screamed. The motivations we were pinning on him were weak.

"Well, thanks. Seeing it is good, I understand how it could have been done. Two injections aren't much, and then Isaac could have slipped away, so he didn't have to watch Georgie die."

"Exactly. Want to see it in the syringe, see what it looks like?"

Alarm bells began to ring in my head. Why on earth did she want to show me that? "Oh no. No, that's fine. It would ruin the bottle, and you'd have to buy more. And it really is getting late. I must be going home."

"To that detective?" Chloe asked, distractedly opening the largest syringe. The harsh white light of the pharmacy glinted on the sharp tip of the needle, and a cold bead of sweat ran between my shoulder blades. I clutched the handle of my handbag tighter and wished Loki had stuck around. Not that I was sure he would help me.

"To my cats," I said, realising my mistake too late. Nobody was expecting me home. I believed Chloe had thrown that brick through my window more than ever. But something else was pricking my brain. If she was capable of that, what else was she capable of?

The image of smiling, bushy-eyebrowed Charlie swam into my vision: *"So, like I said, I doubt it was a theft."*

He hadn't thought the morphine was stolen. But he hadn't gone so far as to say it was an inside job. But what if it was? What if a member of staff had stolen the bottle or even switched it over?

"What are you doing?" I asked, gasping as I realised Chloe was drawing the morphine into the syringe.

"Like I said, showing you."

"No, Chloe, I have to go now. But thank you. This has been great. We should do it again sometime."

I ran for the door. I was too slow.

Fast as lightning Chloe leapt over the counter and threw herself at me. We slammed into the door, with my face pressed hard against the thick glass panel.

"Since you seem so interested in poking your damn nose in, I'm showing you how it happened. How that old cretin met his end. Just like you're about to. His body would have turned to jelly. His mind would have turned to mush."

Desperately I kicked out and shimmied my body from side to side as I tried to knock her off my back. Several times I felt the sharp scratch of the needle at the skin of my neck, and I rocked harder, dislodging her but never enough to toss her off completely.

"Stop squirming!" she complained.

"Why would I stop, idiot?" I said through gritted teeth.

Beside me, a hiss exploded like an open gas main. At first, I thought there was a gas leak, but the hiss was followed up with pounding pawsteps as Loki launched himself at Chloe and grabbed the syringe out of her hands. The plastic crunched between his jaws, and he was lucky he was already dead, or the morphine dose would have killed him all over.

"What the–" Chloe asked, finally sitting up and relieving the pressure on my back.

I took the opportunity to push her off and stood up, dusting myself off. "That's karma."

Chloe blinked up at me. Even beaten, she was able to look snarky. "Me? You must be joking. Georgie was the one who got karma. I dish out the karma. Me. Not you."

Technically, it had been Loki, but since she couldn't see him, I decided to take the credit for destroying the morphine vial.

Chloe didn't seem in a hurry to try a new attack, so I used my advantage of being on my feet to rush behind the counter toward the back exit. The door rattled on its hinges as I tried the doorknob.

"Locked," Chloe called a note of pride in her voice.

No wonder she was in no rush to make a second attempt on my life. She had me trapped.

"Mrow," Loki said, appearing before me and heading left.

Stock room! Maybe I could barricade myself in there and call for help? Or climb out a window? "Good boy, Loki."

I hurried inside and slammed the door behind me. The room was small, narrow and dark. No window, but a light bulb of approximately one-point-three watts hung sadly on a wire above my head to enable me just about to make out my hand in front of my face. There was no lock on the door, so I spun around and strode into the small room, hoping to find something heavy to push against the door.

After no more than two steps, I tripped over something in the darkness.

Something that grunted.

I screamed.

Thirty-Two

Well that went terribly. Certainly not my fault, I blame poor planning.

Once again I had to come to my human's rescue, otherwise that morphine stuff would have plunged into her. From all accounts that seems to be a bad thing, so I went out of my way to help. She is still alive, so I think my part has been very successful.

If only everybody could be as brilliant as me, just think how far we could progress as a planet.

--Thoughts from Loki

I screamed again for good measure, then when nothing happened, I crouched down and used the torch on my phone to investigate the lightly groaning lump I had nearly tripped over.

"Charlie?" I asked as the silver-blue light illuminated his haggard, pale face.

His dilated pupils attempted to focus on my face without great success.

"Mother?" he asked drowsily.

"Uh, most certainly not," I said, making a mental note to moisturise more.

The door opened to the stock room, and Chloe leaned against the doorframe, haloed with light. "Well, this is awkward."

"What have you done to Charlie?" I demanded.

"Morphine. It seems to be my weapon of choice, so I thought I'd stick with it."

"You're killing your boss?" I asked. "You are going to be so fired."

"As if I care!"

"Why?" I asked.

Chloe misinterpreted my question as to why she had done this to Charlie as an invitation to reveal her master plan. In true Bond villain style, lauding over the hero because she knew there was no way they could escape and cause her confession to have consequences. She even took a moment to enter the room and crouched next to me to get more comfortable.

"I saw you, you know? When I was doing my teeth in the mirror. I could see you over my shoulder with the notebook. I don't know how you knew I'd written the confession note, but I couldn't let you take it. That note will be found but only when I'm ready."

Confession note? What was she on about? I'd just wanted to see if she'd chucked a brick through my window. Had I accidentally stumbled onto something more sinister?

"It's fine. You can pay for a new window," I said.

"It's so much more than the window, though, right?"

Honestly, I thought compensation for the window was enough, but I could see she was leading up to something more important, so I let her continue. Especially as I had no idea if she had another vial of morphine hidden up her sleeve.

"I did that to my best friend. I betrayed him, knowing that he was so trusting. I switched out the bottles, you see? When Isaac came to pick up the medication, I had tipped the lower dose of morphine down the sink and filled it up with the high-strength stuff, knowing that Isaac often gave Georgie more than he was meant to have. That poor boy always did as he was told. He was so scared of losing his job."

"And now he's going to prison."

"I said I'd look after him," she shot back. "I always promised to look after him, but he was the one who screwed up his life. He failed his exams but still wanted to be a nurse to make his parents proud. Did he think he wouldn't get prison time for impersonating a nurse and taking medical jobs? It would come out eventually."

"But it might not have been a fatal mistake."

Chloe hesitated, her teeth worrying her lower lip and scraping off more purple lipstick. This time I didn't bother wasting words telling her that she had lipstick on her teeth again. She wouldn't fall for that trick twice.

"I *will* look after him. That's why I wrote the confession note. He won't rot in prison, the police will find that letter and know the truth, and he'll be released. He really didn't do anything; he had no idea I switched the morphine. But first, I'm going to sort out this inheritance thing, then I'll leave town, hell I'll leave the country like that damn swindler did, and I'll leave my confession note so they can release Isaac. And by then, I'll be far away and living my best life on a beach just like he did."

"Until you're extradited. Just like *he* was."

I thought the comparison of her and Georgie would be enough to set her into a violent rage, but instead, the fight seemed to leave her. Her shoulders slumped, and her cat-like green gaze fell on Charlie, whose chest was heaving.

"I know. But what am I supposed to do? I thought I'd gotten on with my life, but when he was released from prison and came here, it was like someone had ripped open all the wounds I had worked so hard to mend. It was all everyone coming into the pharmacy could talk about, and every time I heard his name, it was like another knife to the gut. My father killed himself because of that monster. I never even met him. I have no photos of him holding me. That piece of filth stole my family from me."

So this was all a mistake. I'd come expecting to find evidence that Chloe had broken my window and threatened an officer of the law and found instead her signed confession of murder. But too early. She wasn't ready to share it, and now Charlie and I would be silenced.

"But why Charlie?" I asked.

"Bad timing. I was supposed to be the only one in this evening. I was writing my confession note when Charlie came back. He was still thinking about the damn missing morphine and wanted to ask me again about it. If he'd just let it go,"

"You'll kill an innocent man for doing the right thing?"

"No!" she hissed, her eyes narrowing. "I revised my plan. I was going to leave the country right away and work on getting that inheritance from overseas. On my way out, I'd call for an ambulance. They'd get here and administer the Naloxone antidote, and Charlie'd be fine. I wasn't going to let him die."

I had no reason not to believe her, which made me feel a little better. "Once you'd fled the country, it would be pretty hard to get the inheritance."

"I didn't say plan B was a good plan."

"So what's plan C?"

"Plan C was morphine for you, too," she said. "But that didn't work, so I'm onto plan D."

"You're running out of letters. What's plan D?"

"I'm still figuring it out!" Chloe snapped.

Just as Charlie gave an almighty gasp, then his chest fell still.

Thirty-Three

Oh my, this is certainly not going to plan at all. More thought should have been put into the planning section of this plan.

Now we have another corpse on our hands, although fresh. Perhaps it can be saved. I can see the soul straining against the flesh, they don't have long if they're going to do something to fix this.

--Thoughts from Loki

"Plan D," I suggested. "Save Charlie's life."

"Oh god, oh god. I didn't mean to kill him." Her hand flew to her mouth, long nails digging into the skin around her lips as she watched the colour drain from Charlie's face.

"We can't give up yet. I'll do CPR, and you call an ambulance."

"He needs Naloxone," Chloe said.

"He needs an ambulance!"

"I can't! I can't leave until I know he's okay, but if the ambulance comes, they'll want to know why he had the morphine in his system. I need to be far, far away by then."

"Chloe, call the damn ambulance!" I cried again as I got into position on my knees beside Charlie and began chest compressions.

My heart was pounding, and blood was pumping in my ears, but still, I could clearly hear Chloe rifling through the shelves and knocking boxes to the floor in her haste to find the antidote. I could distinctly *not* hear her calling for help.

"Loki! Loki phone," I called, hoping that at least my ghost cat would do as I damn well asked.

My wrists and upper arms were already starting to ache from the force of the compressions, and distantly I tried to remember the ratio to breaths.

Loki finally appeared and nudged my phone toward me.

"Can you dial?" I asked.

He rightly looked at me as if I were insane.

"Fine, I'll do everything."

As I dipped to breathe into Charlie's mouth and pinch his nose with one hand, the other reached out to unlock my screen and dial 999. I stuck it on speakerphone and returned to the compressions.

"999, which service do you require?"

"Ambulance."

The line went quiet for a moment, then was picked up by a male voice. *"Is the patient breathing?"*

"No, I'm doing CPR on him." My voice strained from the effort. Good god, how did people do this for minutes and minutes on end?

"Found it!" Chloe said as she raced into the store room and dropped to her knees.

"What address are you calling from?" asked my phone.

"You called an ambulance? What did I tell you? I can fix this!" Chloe said.

"Charles Gibson Pharmacy, in Catton Strawless," I shouted.

"Postcode?"

"Google it," Chloe snapped and swiped to end the call on my phone.

"Chloe, what are you doing?"

"Saving his life."

She sat back on her heels and measured out a dose of Naloxone from the small clear bottle she had brought with her. Carefully she flicked the syringe to remove air bubbles, then pulled down Charlie's shirt shoulder and sank the needle into his arm.

I removed my hands from his chest but was instantly pushed over.

"Don't stop!" Chloe said, but instead of letting me continue, she took over the compressions.

"But you just gave him the antidote."

"That won't bring him back. We still need to get his heart going."

Chloe was much better at the compressions than I was. Her arms pressed down rhythmically, short and sharp, never missing a beat. Every few presses, she dipped her head to force air into Charlie's mouth, then would start the cycle all over again.

She continued for what felt like forever.

Fear crept over me like an icy fog, convincing me he wasn't coming back from this. Every second that passed was a second closer to that realisation, but Chloe gave no indication she was ready to give up.

"Come on, come on," she muttered as she pushed hard, willing Charlie back to us.

The first twitch of his fingers, I thought I imagined. The second was accompanied by a sharp intake of breath, and then Charlie's large body spasmed.

"Oh god," Chloe said, falling back on her butt and wiping sweaty blue hair from her eyes. But there was a relieved smile on her lips, a more relaxed pose to her shoulders.

"You did it," I said. Then realised my mistake. "I mean, you caused it in the first place."

"I nearly killed him," Chloe said.

"Yeah, you did. But he's alive." I pointed to the coughing, curled-up form of her boss. Yeah, she was so fired.

Chloe wasn't done, though. "And I did that to Isaac. I made him a murderer. He didn't know it, but now he has to live with it for the rest of his life, knowing he injected the fatal dose. He took a life. And I tricked him into doing it. I thought it wasn't a crime. That Weaver deserved it. And he was dying anyway; he was a sick old man. It didn't feel like a crime, but that was because it wasn't me that did it, wasn't it? Being brave is easy when you're not the one doing it. I'm not brave. I'm not clever. I'm a coward."

"Chloe?" I asked after what felt like a respectable pause to allow her to reflect on her revelation.

"Yeah?" she asked softly.

"Do you think we need to check on Charlie?"

"Oh right, yeah." Chloe grabbed her jacket from the coat peg and tucked it around the shivering man.

I blinked. The hood. The dark jacket. Chloe had been there in the crowds, silently plotting how to kill Georgie all along.

"What was that stuff you gave him?" I asked.

"Naloxone. It reverses opioid overdoses. It's pretty fast acting. He'll feel weird for a few more hours but should wear off after a day or two."

"Wow. That's amazing you knew what to use."

"Yeah, almost like I'm a pharmacist. Go figure," she said sarcastically, then her shoulders slumped and she heaved a sigh. "Not that all my knowledge is going to be much use in prison."

In the distance, an ambulance siren was wailing, getting closer to us. They had taken Chloe's advice and googled the address.

"You could still go," I said, watching her carefully. "Charlie will be ok now. You could head off and get out of the country. May I suggest somewhere without extradition deals? Start fresh and put everything behind you. You won't have the inheritance money, but you'll be free."

Slowly she shook her head. The roots of her dark hair were starting to show beneath the vibrant blue. I had a vision of them growing out even longer, of her wearing a prison uniform.

"I'm not going anywhere. What I did was wrong. Even if I tried to justify it, I'm not sad Weaver is dead, but I know I shouldn't have done it. The worst thing, though, is using Isaac to do it. Maybe I could live with myself if it was just Weaver on my conscience but not Isaac. The thought of him living with what I did to him and me not being punished in any way would eat me alive. I get that now."

"So what next?"

"We wait. The ambulance will be here soon. They'll call the police. They'll arrest me and let Isaac go free. That's how it should be."

Perhaps her conscience was clearing as she could lift her head and meet my gaze. I realised she had started referring to Georgie as "Weaver" rather than tosser, cretin, or other more colourful terms. Perhaps that was part of the healing process, too, that he was no longer the monster of her nightmares, the boogie man who had stolen her father.

"You're wrong," I said. "You're not a coward."

"I'm working on it."

We unlocked the front door, and paramedics worked on Charlie, who was still out of it. He was wheeled out to the waiting ambulance and taken to hospital.

After I called Thomas, we made two cups of tea and sat on the storeroom floor together, just waiting.

The door banged open. Thomas and another officer stormed in with military precision covering both aisles of the pharmacy and securing the area. They then entered the storeroom, kicking open the door to find Chloe and me sitting, chatting, and drinking tea.

"What took you so long? I called fifteen minutes ago," I said.

Thomas seemed momentarily unbalanced and glanced at me, raising a quizzical eyebrow.

"I'm fine. She's giving herself up willingly. You can probably do without the stabproof vests."

"Right. Well, Chloe Samson, I am arresting you on suspicion of the murder of Georgie Weaver."

"Sure. Let me just finish my tea."

Again, Thomas didn't seem to know the proper etiquette for this, so we all just waited in awkward silence while Chloe slurped the last mouthful and set the cup down on the floor.

"Can you tell Charlie I'm sorry I didn't wash the cups up?"

"Yeah, I will," I said.

Chloe rose to her feet and held out her hands. The other officer snapped on handcuffs and led her toward the door with a large hand on her thin shoulder.

Before she left, she turned back to me with a smile. "Thanks."

And then she was gone.

Thomas knelt next to me. "Why on earth is she thanking you?"

"It's complicated."

"This has been an eventful evening. What happened?"

"I'll tell you later. I want to go home and curl up on the sofa with some blankets and something warm to drink."

"Not something stronger?"

"Alcohol is probably the last thing I need."

Thomas raised his eyebrow again. Or had it never really lowered?

"I'll explain later. Can we just go home, please?"

"Of course."

Chloe had left the key on the counter, so we could lock up. At some point, when he was back on his feet, I would return the key to Charlie and explain why his star pharmacist would no longer be working for him.

But that could be another day. Tonight I just wanted to relax, recover and spend time with my cats. And Thomas.

Thirty-Four

All's well that ends well. I heard that somewhere.

Obviously all did not end well for everyone. The convict died. The brutish man is back in prison. The pharmacist will be tried for murder. The nurse who isn't really a nurse now has to explain to his parents.

Hm, perhaps all is not well.

But it certainly seems that Willow and Thomas are coming along nicely. So that's one positive. And the cat café opens tomorrow. Also a positive.

You have to get the positives where you can in this world. Sage still doesn't speak much, though I encouraged her to leave the carrier briefly. She's small, I wonder how young she is.

The only word she says is "onions" though. I tried to bring her one but she shook her head and retreated into the carrier again..

--Thoughts from Luna

Any plans for recreating our first kiss or suggesting Thomas lay in bed with me flew out of the window.

The effort of walking home drained me so that by the time we reached my house, I barely had the strength to lift the key to the lock. Locking the door again behind us seemed a cruel ask, and Thomas did the honours for me.

I groaned and glared at the staircase. "Why don't we put bedrooms on the ground floor?"

"We sometimes do. They're called bungalows."

"I want a bungalow. I don't think I can get up the stairs. Can I sleep here?"

"In the hallway?"

"We let Sage sleep here."

"Sage is a cat," Thomas pointed out.

"I can crawl like a worm. No, they don't crawl, do they? Shimmy. I can shimmy."

"Okay, this is just sad. Let me give you a hand, my little worm."

And then I was flying. Weightless. Like a worm that had metamorphosised into a butterfly. Wait, that's caterpillars, isn't it? Can worms become butterflies? Suddenly this seemed to be a very important question, so I asked Thomas.

"Worms just stay worms all their life."

"That's sad."

"Terribly so."

The flight came to an end when I landed on a cloud. Blankets wrapped around me as if by magic, and I snuggled down into my cocoon. Maybe I was metamorphosising?

"I have questions," I said, realising suddenly that I did indeed have questions.

"You and me both. But we need a good night's sleep before we try to make sense of any of this."

"The café is opening tomorrow."

"I'd forgotten about that. All the more reason to get some sleep."

And so sleep I did. There was no graceful fluttering of eyelids as I drifted peacefully off to the land of nod. I fell unconscious with my mouth open, snoring loudly with a line of drool down my cheek.

Nice.

In the morning, my throat was dry from my mouth being open all night. My shoulders and back creaked and ached from where I had sat on the cold pharmacy storeroom tiles. I padded into the kitchen, rubbing at my sore eyes.

"Good morning," Thomas said.

"Urgh," I answered. "What time is it?"

"Surely you have walked past your phone and several clocks?"

I fixed him with a glare and poured myself a coffee. While still glaring at him.

"Just gone seven," he answered.

"Still time to shower and make the grand opening. I promised to be there by eight. And I need to get the cats ready. Ugh, still so much to do." I drank a gulp of scalding hot coffee, hoping the temperature and caffeine would give me a much-needed boost. They did not. Instead, I just burned my tongue and made myself look an idiot (again) as I coughed, spluttered and hopped around the kitchen, frantically waving a hand in front of my burning mouth.

"Careful, it's hot," Thomas said.

"Thanks," I lisped.

"Anything I can help with?"

"Yes. I need to make a decision. About little miss wallflower in the hallway."

"Sage," Thomas said, nodding as if to confirm my doubts. "She's not ready to be around a lot of people. Sorry to say, she probably won't ever be."

I sat on the corner of the kitchen table, hugging my cup with my hands. "I was thinking the same thing. I suppose two out of three isn't bad; that's what Meatloaf always said. I kind of want to keep her myself, but if I end up taking in all the cats that try out for the café and don't work out, I'm going to end up with a house full of felines."

"It'll be disruptive for her if she goes back to the shelter. She'll feel bad that she didn't get to find a home and confused as to why she's back there. Next time someone takes her home, she might assume she will end up right back again."

My heart sank to my feet like a lead weight, and suddenly I didn't feel like drinking my coffee. The idea that Sage would feel abandoned and unwanted tore at my heart.

"I'll keep her," I heard myself saying. "She will always have a home here."

"Well then, shall I get the two stars of the show packed up in their carriers while you shower?"

My heart moved back to its rightful place just in time to melt. "Thank you."

"You've got to look your best for the cameras."

"Cameras?" I asked, my heart sinking again. Jesus, I was going to need a cardiac operation at this rate.

"You invited a bunch of influencers and media. They'll want some pictures of the owners with the cats."

"Yeah. Yeah. Of course. I knew that." Suddenly my desire for coffee returned, and I downed the entire mug. "I look a mess. After last night I'm surprised I can string a sentence together."

"Just refrain from dropping to the floor and wiggling like a worm, and you'll be fine."

"Oh, damn you! I was senseless with exhaustion!"

Thomas grinned, his cheeks dimpling. "Go on. I'll sort out the cats. You get yourself showered and dressed. And maybe brush your hair?"

Clean. Dressed in a pair of grey skinny jeans, white sneakers and a long-sleeved beige turtle neck sweater, I carried Boo through the doors of The Mews and Beans Cat Café, with Thomas and Bagel following behind.

"You're here!" Pippa squeaked.

"It's only two minutes past eight; I'm barely late at all," I said.

"What cuties! The pictures don't do them justice. Hello little one. Is this Boo?"

"Yes, that's Boo. Careful, the second you open the door, she'll–"

"Wah!" Pippa cried, tumbling from her crouched position onto her backside as Boo made a run for it, doing a lap of the café then leaping onto one of the cat trees and working on batting a wooden fish on a string at high speed.

"Like I said, she's a bit energetic."

"Going to have to watch her. Or put a bell on her," Pippa said. "Dare I open Bagel up?"

"Oh yeah, he'll take forever to come out. He'll go faster if there's the promise of food. He can *really* move if he smells tuna."

Tentatively Pippa unclipped the little wire door on Bagel's door, and, true to form, the tabby slowly plodded out with his nose to the ground sniffing as he went. He roamed right up to Pippa and climbed right into her lap, doing a circle before plopping down and curling in on himself.

"I think he's found a new bed," I laughed.

"This is a terrible idea," Pippa groaned, her fingers running through his thick fur. "I'm never going to get any work done. I'll just be petting cats all day."

"There are worse ways to spend time," I said, crouching beside her and scratching behind Bagel's ears.

The purr that erupted from deep within his throat melted both our hearts.

"I don't mean to interrupt, but shouldn't we be getting ready?" Thomas asked. "People will be arriving soon."

"Yes, right. You are very right. Willow, how do I extract myself?"

I helped her move the warm lump of Bagel and deposited him back on the floor. He was still for a long moment, then began snuffling around, hoping to find a food bowl somewhere. The joke was on him; we would let the influencers pour the first bowls of food in an hour's time, so he would be disappointed even if he found the bowls.

You'd think he hadn't already had breakfast.

Last minute preparations were made, and then myself, Oli and even Thomas were handed brand new aprons in the turquoise and pink colours of the café, with our new logo emblazoned on the breast.

"Uniform," Pippa explained. "Today, we need to look professional. It can make or break us. So I need everyone to smile – Bardot, smile. No, *smile*. You do know what a smile is?"

"I am smiling."

"If that's the best you can do, never mind."

Thomas frowned.

"Better. Ok, guys, this is a big day. A huge day. I have wanted a café since I was little. Other girls wanted to be hairdressers, or doctors, or feng shui consultants – don't ask – but I always played café. I would fill little cups for my stuffed animals and use my little electric oven to make truly awful cookies. But I knew it was the only thing I wanted to do with my life."

"Pippa–"

Pippa held up a hand to silence me. "Let me say this, Willow. My café failed. Because I wanted to make things from scratch and I wanted to give my customers a great experience. But it was a terrible business model because of the time it took for orders to be completed. I couldn't compete with the other cafés with premade sandwiches and sausage rolls ready to go, so people got their lunch from everywhere else.

"I was in financial ruin. I was about to give this place up when Willow, you came up with the idea of a café where people come for the experience as much as the food. People would want to stay here and be willing to wait. And Bardot, you offered the money to make this rebrand happen. I can't thank you both enough. I promise to do my best to make this the best damn café in the UK."

Oli clapped loudly, and Thomas joined in. I threw myself at Pippa in a hug, pulling her close. "Silly, we're in this together now. We'll both work hard to make it work out."

"Thank you, Willow."

"Come on, guys. People will be arriving soon. Last minute preparation, then we're live," Oli said with a wicked smile. "So, no pressure, eh?"

Exactly. It was just the only thing Pippa had dreamed of her whole life. No pressure, indeed.

Thirty-Five

Luna is trying to help and I do appreciate it. But she doesn't understand. Nobody can understand. I like Luna though, she's comforting like a mother. I hope she never leaves me. Everyone else leaves me.

I miss Onion.

--Thoughts from Sage

My back ached. My feet ached. My ear lobes ached.

But it was a damn good ache.

Cat treats littered the floor, trodden to dust by dozens of excited pairs of feet as they angled to get the best photos of the cats.

Someone had spilt their tea, and there was now a sticky patch near the counter that needed mopping up before Bagel took it upon himself to lick it clean.

Dirty plates, cups and glasses piled high on the table nearest the staff-only door, waiting to be carried through and loaded into the dishwasher.

Did I care? Not one bit.

The opening morning had been a roaring success. The influencers had posed with the cats, making instant friends with Bagel and Boo, feeding them treats, giving them cuddles, and petting them while they worked on their laptops. The local news covered it all, showing how you could work, enjoy a snack and play with the cats.

Pippa gave an amazing recorded interview, during which Bagel curled on her lap and did his best to look as adorable as possible, including his signature bagel "O" tail.

Now the door was closed, and everyone had gone home to post, share and comment to build up the hype. From tomorrow we would be open to the public and find out if this crazy idea would actually bring in customers. We might even need a booking system, I'd have to look into that.

"They enjoyed themselves," Thomas said, running a hand over Bagel's spine as the lazy tabby sidled up next to him.

We were all sat on a rug by the large window, each one of us exhausted but smiling. Bagel had lapped up the attention but was starting to tire. Boo was still curiously exploring each of the cat trees, jumping between them with energy to spare.

"They did. I'm so glad," Pippa said. "Good choices on the cats, Willow."

"Well, two out of three. Sage isn't going to be a café cat. She's far too shy. I couldn't put her in here. She'd be scared of all the attention and noise."

"That's a shame. But these two little guys are naturals."

I was about to say something, nothing particularly important, when a shadow loomed tall in the frosted glass door. The figure hesitated and then pushed, only to find the door was locked. Not to be deterred, they rapped their knuckles on the glass.

"We're closed," Pippa yelled.

The figure knocked again.

"Not taking no for an answer," I said with an eye roll. "I'll point him to another place to get their coffee fix."

Standing up, my knees clicked painfully, and my feet buzzed as the circulation returned to them. Feeling about eighty years old, I made my way to the door, pulled the bar lock and opened the door, ready to apologise and put them on their way.

"Isaac?" I said.

"Uh yeah. I just wanted to stop by."

"Of course, come in."

I stood aside and locked the door behind him. He shuffled across the floor, seemingly unsure what to do with his long, lanky body. One hand encircled the other wrist as he turned to Thomas.

"They let me go this morning. Said no reason to keep me, but they may need to ask some more questions later."

"Yes, they might," Thomas said, his voice even and calm.

"They were asking me things about Chloe. Weird things. They said she switched out the morphine, so the stuff I injected Georgie with was way stronger?"

"That's what she confessed to."

"Why would she do that?"

Switch the medication or confess? It was hard to tell what he was asking. I placed a hand on his shoulder and felt his body tense.

"She did it for you. She promised she'd look after you, right? Just take this as the gift she intended. She got her revenge, and you got your freedom."

Isaac collapsed onto the floor, his legs folding like origami. He buried his face in his hands and rocked gently back and forth. "Doesn't make any sense. He was dying anyway."

"Not fast enough," I said, crouching next to him. "And not by her hand. She wanted to be the one to snuff out his life."

"How could she?" Isaac asked. His eyes were rimmed red when he drew his hands away from his face.

"She felt she had to. But she didn't want to hurt you, so she did the right thing in the end. She gave herself up and made sure you were set free."

"Isaac, the important thing is she could have run off. She could have left the country, never to be seen again. But because you were in trouble, she gave up her own freedom. So don't waste that. Sure, everyone knows you aren't a registered nurse, but there are worse things. At least you're not a convicted murderer. See this as a second chance and get back on track. Find a new career. Make something of your life. For yourself. For Chloe. Otherwise, she might as well have vanished last night."

He swallowed hard, his adam's apple bobbing. For a second, when he drew a deep breath, I thought he would burst into tears. He swiped the back of his hand under his nose and nodded to himself.

"Yeah. Yeah. I can...maybe become an engineer? I could go back to uni and–"

"Or maybe an apprenticeship or something?" I suggested. He had zero money to pay for another university course.

"Yeah, maybe that. I haven't decided yet," Isaac said, his gaze returning to his hands, which were fiddling with the hem of his sleeves.

Thomas opened his mouth, perhaps to suggest a trade that might suit Isaac, when Boo scurried up, her little claws scratching on the floor and leapt into Isaac's lap.

"Whoa there!" he acted fast to grab her before she tumbled off his bony knees and held her close as she reached up her paws to his chest and began licking his stubble of a beard.

"Boo has faith in you," I said.

"I love cats. Have you got cats here now? Are you sure I can't have a job here?"

"Sorry, kiddo, we're just starting out," Pippa said.

Isaac's shoulders relaxed as he ran gentle fingers over Boo's cream fur. She tilled and purred at the attention, flopping onto her back and submitting to belly scratches in a calm way she never did with anyone else.

"Hey, you have a way with her. She never stays still for me," I said.

"I've always been good with animals. They don't talk back like patients do."

Now I know why they call it a lightbulb moment. I could literally hear the click of the light switching on in my brain as if my mind was illuminated with understanding. "A shelter! Why don't you work at a shelter? Or work in a vets? I'm not sure if you can ever qualify after you...you know...lied about being a nurse. But you can still get a job there with animals."

His face lit up, and the lines in his forehead melted away to reveal the youth I had seen when he first appeared in Catton Strawless.

"I could work with animals. Yeah, I could do that. That would be awesome. It would be fun."

"Well, there you go."

"Thank you. I should go. I need to call my mum. She was worried sick when she found out I was arrested. Now I can explain. And I can tell her I have a new plan. She doesn't have to worry about me."

"I think mums will always worry about their kids, no matter how old they are. Or what dumb things they do." I said.

After a few more cuddles, Isaac plucked a reluctant Boo from his lap and left, looking brighter and happier than ever. Hopefully, a more promising future lay ahead of him. The past had certainly not been kind.

"Oh, by the way, check this out," Pippa said, holding her phone to me with a social media profile. "Meet Elizabeth Phelps, or Lizzie as she likes to be called. Look familiar?"

The picture was of a fit, youthful woman in a bikini with blonde curls and a cocktail in hand as she lounged on a beach.

The hair hadn't been dyed red, and the makeup was more garish, but there was no mistaking it.

"Maria Weaver. Caught out," I said.

"Yup, total fraud. She has nothing to do with Georgie. This looks like the real Maria Weaver. She lives in Australia now with a wife and two pugs. Took her wife's name and looks like she has completely abandoned her English life."

Another profile, this time a woman with short-cropped red hair, a deep tan and a nose ring. Not only that, she was much shorter and curvier than Lizzie and had a more casual fashion sense.

"Well, Thomas?" I asked.

"Not my department, but I'll make sure the proper checks are done and that Ms Phelps gets her just rewards," Thomas said, a smirk on his lips as he imagined the horrid woman who had interrupted us in our nightwear and demanded an interview.

"So sad," I said, placing a hand over my heart. "Actually, I'm over it. So does that mean the real Maria will get the money?"

"I guess. They'll trace her and make contact. Surprised they hadn't already, but she had changed her name. Pippa that was some awesome detective work to find her."

Pippa shrugged but couldn't help the proud smile that tugged at her lips. "What can I say?"

"Thomas, admit it. You need us. That's two murders that we've solved for you."

"Excuse me?"

"Well, I was the one who got the confession note. It was my plan all along to draw her out."

Thomas rolled his eyes. "You mean you stumbled in, could have got yourself killed and got damn lucky. Again."

"Yes, that's what I said," I smiled sweetly. "Well, next time–"

"No no. No no no," Pippa rose to her knees and held up her hands. "There will not be a next time. This is Catton Strawless, the sleepiest town in the sleepiest county. We don't have murders every other week; we're not bloody London. We've had our quota of deaths to see us through until I'm long and buried."

"It doesn't quite work like that," Thomas said.

"Yes, it does. Because this town is beautiful and quaint and *not* a murder capital. I can't use that in my advertising!"

"Cat-ostrophically good coffee," Oli said.

"Fur-raisingly good paninis," I suggested.

"Not you, too," Pippa said, glaring at her boyfriend first, then me.

"Purr-fectly criminal doughnuts," Thomas said.

"No. No no. No more murders. No more deaths. This is it. A new chapter for our little town and a new café for people to come far and wide to see," Pippa insisted. "To the future!"

I raised my empty coffee cup in a toast. "I can drink to that. To the future."

The others raised their cups, the four mugs clinking as they met.

As I pretended to drink from my empty mug, I caught Thomas' gaze. His smile melted me like chocolate in a fondant pot.

Yes. To the future, indeed.

The End

Read the rest of the series now!

If you want to be the first to know when a new release is out, why not sign up for my mailing list? Plus you'll get a free short story "Bardot's Christmas Case": **https://dl.bookfunnel.com/vn72feoo33**

Thank you for reading! If you enjoyed the book I would be very grateful if you would consider leaving a review. It is really helpful for independent authors to get feedback and to help other readers discover our books.

Until next time!
www.sarahmaybirdbooks.com

Cat Café Mystery Novels
Feline Deadly
Furgotten Felonies
Paw Prints of Murder
Claws of Suspicion
Bad Cattitude
Pawtrait of a Killer

Cat Café Shorts

A Christmas Yowl

Purranormal Cattivity

Loki Investigates Trilogy Mystery Novels

A Fur-Midable Team

A Tail of Truth

Justice Fur All

Made in United States
North Haven, CT
10 February 2026